The Buffalo Gun

Arrow Ridge was a cattle town with most of its sprawling ranges owned or appropriated by Clay Glandon, ruthless boss of the Big Three outfit. Newly arrived homesteaders were being harassed and driven off their land by Glandon's men, and only Tom Cardigan's outfit, the TT, was prepared to stand up and fight for what was theirs.

When lone rider Will Keever arrived in the town, all eyes there noted the powerful buffalo gun he carried in its scabbard, and those with reason to fear retribution were immediately uneasy – and especially so when they learned his name, for Keever's reputation as a gunslinger had preceded him. He was a man on a mission and that mission would bring him into deadly conflict with Glandon.

By the same author

Lonesome Gun
Six-Gun Prodigal

The Buffalo Gun

Ken Brompton

A Black Horse Western

ROBERT HALE · LONDON

ISBN 978-0-7090-8652-9

Robert Hale Limited
Clerkenwell House
Clerkenwell Green
London EC1R 0HT

www.halebooks.com

Typeset by
Derek Doyle & Associates, Shaw Heath
Printed and bound in Great Britain by
CPI Antony Rowe, Chippenham, Wiltshire

CHAPTER ONE

MYSTERIOUS RIDER

Almost nothing was left of the small vegetable garden fronting the homesteaders' cabin within five minutes of the eight horsemen starting to maul it under the hoofs of their mounts. The slashing rain aided the destruction as the wide-hatted riders, huddled in slickers and range-blankets, whooped and hollered and trampled the earth and vegetation into a morass of mud by circling their animals again and again.

The night sky was black and moonless and out of it deluged the rain, the merciless rain of these

Montana rangelands, fit to make any thinking man from elsewhere wonder why he ever sought a life here and probably set even the Indians to feeling there must be better places to be born.

Nevertheless, homesteaders had arrived with high hopes of building their future by farming the land and raising their families here.

But there were others, already on the scene, with different ideas. They claimed a prior right to these ranges exclusively for the cattle they ran. They wanted the homesteaders to be gone and one set of incomers was now feeling the destructive power of their determination.

At first, when the riders came pounding out of the night, the homesteader showed yellow lamplight in his cabin window. The raiders got down to business at once, screeching and charging their mounts across the vegetable patch, hauling rein, swinging their animals about and walking them back and to across the cultivated plot.

Startled faces appeared at the window – the homesteader, his wife and a couple of small children.

'Get off my land!' came a man's voice in querulous protest from behind the glass.

'Your land be damned! This is Big Three range, always has been and always will be. Get the hell back to where you came from or be burned out!' hooted the slicker-wrapped man who headed the raiders. He was Dan Flagel, foreman of the Big Three, a cattle outfit that hogged a vast acreage of these ranges.

'We're here legally under the Homestead Act, with title to the land,' came the thin voice from behind the rain-streaked window.

Flagel answered by producing from under his slicker a hand filled with his Colt .45 and blasting a shot which sent a chip spinning out of the log wall close to the window. He loosed a second bullet with similar effect. 'Get the hell out!' he yelled, as the sound of the shooting clattered off over the empty land.

At once, the lamplight in the cabin was doused.

Another rider, blanketed against the downpour and with the wide chaps of the region flapping against his legs, nudged his horse up against Flagel's. 'How many's in there, Dan?' he asked, from under a dripping hat-brim pulled down almost to his nose.

'Four, I hear. Man, wife and two kids.'

'There's a lean-to stable in back. We could set a fire in it and that'll clear 'em out quick enough.'

'No,' said Flagel. 'There'll be a wagon in there and they'll need it for travelling tomorrow because

7

they'll sure enough get out tomorrow. Give 'em a few more shots to scare 'em, then let's get out of this damned rain back to some grub and hot coffee.' He returned his sixgun to the holster under his slicker and repeated confidently, 'They'll sure enough get out tomorrow.'

Flagel pranced his horse backwards, and four of his companions fired half-a-dozen more revolver shots at the front of the homestead. Then the Big Three raiding party turned and, huddled over their saddle-horns, departed into the curtains of rain.

Will Keever had the look of a working cowman, though he lacked the chaps usual on these northern ranges. He was gaunt and weather-punished with a black hat yanked forward over dark, vigilant eyes. He wore a slicker, open now since the rain had stopped and there was a warming spread of sunshine. A Peacemaker Colt was visible at his right hip when the slight morning breeze curled back one side of his slicker. It was noted with a certain apprehension by the few townsfolk abroad in Arrow Ridge, as was the butt of the weapon, covered with thick waterproof fabric and housed in his saddle-scabbard, a heavy weapon, possibly a buffalo gun.

He was mounted on a trail-weary roan, burdened with the warsack and bedroll of a travelling man, and the animal paced slowly down the unlovely straggle of the town's single street. The way was fouled by horses and raked by wheel-ruts that brimmed with water from the previous night's rain. Like many another settlement of the northern plains, Arrow Ridge had mushroomed from nothing when the cowmen and their herds took over the land, and its ugly false-fronted wooden buildings and battered plankwalks now showed the weathering of blistering summers and marrow-chilling winters.

'Not a place to spend much time in, hoss,' Keever muttered to his mount. 'Not that we aim to.'

Seeing an old man leaning against a hitch rack, Keever swung out of his saddle and walked his horse across the street to ease the animal. His boots squelched in the soft earth as he approached the onlooker. The old-timer, with a pipe jutting from under a straggle of moustache, eyed him apprehensively. Keever nodded to him.

'Howdy. Any hotels and livery stables here?' he asked.

Around his pipe, the old man said, 'Only one of each, both a little ways ahead of you. The hotel is what I reckon might be called of middling quality. The livery's opposite it and I figure your horse will have the best bargain. Jake Timmins who operates the stable knows horses and keeps a good place.' He considered Keever's gaunt appearance and added for good measure, 'There's an eating-house next to the hotel. Grub there ain't too bad.'

A lean, ferret-faced man with a deputy marshal's star on his buckskin vest, who had observed Keever for some time, strolled up the plankwalk and stood behind the old man. He nodded to Keever and offered a frosty smile. 'New in town?' he asked.

'Now that you call attention to it, I find I am,' Keever answered flatly.

The deputy swallowed uncertainly, but his curiosity was undiminished. 'Just passing through?' he ventured.

'Yes, heading north.'

The deputy smiled his chilly smile again. 'If you go much further north, you'll wind up in Canada,' he said.

'Sure, well maybe I'm about to take a look at how things are in Canada,' Keever replied. 'Then again, maybe I'll stop short this side of the border.' His flat tone plainly meant: *Where I'm going is none of your damned business.*

Like a man proceeding cautiously over thin ice,

the lawman said, 'I thought maybe you'd showed up to work for Mr Glandon on the Big Three. That's a big cattle outfit, some distance out of town, y'know. Mr Glandon owns it. I thought you might need directions.'

'I don't, since I'm not headed there. And I've heard of the Big Three and of Mr Clay Glandon,' responded Keever. 'I heard about people being run off their homesteads, too. As a matter of fact, I met a family of them back along the trail soon after dawn – man, wife, kids and furniture all crammed on a buckboard.'

The deputy closed down his smile and swallowed again. 'Well, enjoy your stay,' he said without warmth. He walked some distance along the planked sidewalk and Keever watched him stride through a door marked TOWN MARSHAL.

The old man chuckled deep in his throat. 'That was Sam Twigg. He just can't wait to tell his boss, Marshal Wallis, about you.'

He was perfectly correct for, at that very moment, Twigg was standing in front of the desk behind which reposed Marshal Rufe Wallis, a beefy, florid man. Twigg talked rapidly and with a marked degree of edginess.

'. . . tall fellow with a Peacemaker and a damned big thing like a buffalo gun in his scabbard,' he was

11

saying. 'Could be a bounty hunter. Maybe he's even looking for someone among those guys Mr Glandon's been hiring. He's not about to work for Mr Glandon, though. I found out that much.'

'Who Mr Glandon hires is his business,' said the marshal tartly, as if his deputy was touching on a sore subject, 'so forget about the Big Three crew. You didn't get his name, I suppose.'

'No, but then he said he was only passing through,' said Sam Twigg.

'That may be, but he sure enough got you all alarmed, Sam – and he's got me plumb curious, too,' responded the marshal.

'You don't figure Tom Cardigan, out at the TT, has hired him on, do you?' ventured the deputy.

Marshal Wallis gave a braying laugh. 'Cardigan? No, I don't!' he growled emphatically. 'Tom Cardigan and the TT are on their knees and damned near finished. Pretty soon, Cardigan won't be able to buy a flyswatter for self-protection, let alone pay some gunslick.'

Out on the street, the old man took his pipe from his mouth and jabbed its stem towards Keever. 'I'm plumb pleased to know you're not about to work for Glandon, mister,' he said. 'But take a warning from me – don't cross Marshal Wallis or Twigg or Glandon while you're here.

They're all the one kind, Glandon being the biggest damned sidewinder of the three.'

'Thanks for the advice,' said Keever in his colourless way.

The old-timer said cautiously, 'I liked the cool way you dealt with Twigg and I figure the running off of homesteaders don't sit any better with you than it does with me. Do you have a name?'

'Sure I do. Doesn't everybody?' Keever answered. Whereupon, he yanked the rein of his horse and walked it off in search of the livery stable and the hotel, leaving the old man wondering.

Leading the roan through the doorway of the livery stable, he found the proprietor, a small, elderly man, clearing straw from a stall.

'Feed him, give him a drink, brush him and bed him for one night,' he stipulated.

'Sure thing, sir,' grinned the man. 'He'll get the best in the house. Good oats and good, clean bedding. Never had a cayuse complain about our service yet.'

Keever strode the boardwalk, humping his warsack and carrying the big, waterproofed weapon taken from his saddle-scabbard. Again, he was aware of townsfolk openly staring at him, a good deal of their attention obviously being taken by the covered firearm. He found the restaurant. It was empty save for a heavily built man and his scrawny wife, standing behind the counter. Their eyes went to his carried weapon as soon as he entered.

He sat at a table and the man came over from the counter, gave an uncertain smile and asked, 'What'll it be?'

'Something substantial and some good, hot coffee,' replied Keever.

'How about beef, potatoes, beans, sweetcorn and gravy? The missus makes a good apple pie for dessert, too.'

'Fine,' said Keever. When it arrived, the food proved surprisingly good and the coffee was strong and fortifying. He had a second helping of the pie and the couple seemed to see that as his setting a seal of approval on their establishment.

He paid his score and thanked the couple. After he left, the proprietor asked his spouse, 'Another of them suspicious gunhands, headed for the Big Three, d'you think?'

She shrugged. 'Can't say, but he has gentle-manly manners – and he appreciates good cook-ing.'

Keever entered the hotel and found its atmos-phere hardly prepossessing. The place was proba-bly built when Arrow Ridge had ambitions, before it became a mere run-down cowtown, and visitors must be rare. The lobby was empty save for a bald gnome of a man with glasses on the end of his nose who guarded the desk. His gaze, too, was immediately attracted to the covered weapon in the newcomer's hand. He jerked into action when Keever said, 'I'd like a room for one night. Any facilities for a man to take a bath here?'

'You've come to the right place, mister.' The clerk produced a key and handed it over. 'Take number twenty-two, second floor. Bathroom at the end of the passage and there's an oil-burner in there so you can get hot water.'

Keever mounted creaking stairs with the distinct feeling that he was the only guest in the hotel. He found the room, spartan in its furnishings but acceptable enough and, after he lit its wick with a match, the oil-burning device in the bathroom produced enough hot water to allow him the luxury of a bath.

After several nights of sleeping under the stars, open-range style, he fell gratefully into bed. Hitting the pillow, he thought, *Arrow Ridge, a lousy town in dangerous country and Mr Glandon, of the Big Three, is the almighty power here. I get the notion he owns this town or most of it. He probably owns this place too and I could be adding to his profit by staying here. Oh, well, he's welcome to my patronage before I get down to more serious matters with him.*

At which point, he fell into a solid sleep.

He awoke early, washed and, for the first time in nearly a week, shaved. He hauled his warsack and the intriguing weapon down to the desk, paid his bill and was about to depart when the gnome of a clerk called, 'Excuse me, mister. You didn't sign the register last night.' He shoved a battered book across the counter, open at a page significantly blank. Keever had not encountered a single fellow guest and mused that it must count as an event when the hotel sheltered any visitors.

Well, I'll make this an event to remember, he thought.

He took the pen and wrote in a large, clear hand *Will Keever* and added *Apache Wells, Arizona Territory* as his place of residence.

The clerk turned the register around, read it and his Adam's apple rose and fell as he gulped. Over the top of his glasses, he considered Keever not a little fearfully.

Keever asked casually, 'How does a man find the TT ranch? I hear it's north of town.'

The clerk gulped again a couple of times. 'S-sure. North on the main trail, then there's a left fork maybe two miles out of t-town,' he replied, trying to control the stutter that had suddenly afflicted him.

16

'Thanks,' said Keever amiably. He walked out, suppressing a grin of satisfaction until he was on the street, heading for the restaurant. *Now I figure all Arrow Ridge will know my name almost before I saddle up,* he told himself.

Again, he was the restaurant's only customer. The couple welcomed him like a valued patron and he demolished a breakfast of bacon, beans and coffee. Then he collected his rested and refreshed roan at the livery stable and rode north.

The sharp air held the promise of spring. The last hint of rain had cleared and the sun was yet low at this early hour. Life was still hardly stirring on the main street as he followed its length to where it quickly petered out and became a wide trail.

The trail ribboned over wide-open, treeless land, rising slightly ahead of him. Keever found the left fork and took it then, after some time, encountered a board nailed to a wooden post. It bore the painted initials 'TT' and an arrow pointing ahead. He followed the trail upward to where it ran between two shouldering humps of land, rising suddenly out of the flatness of the plain.

After riding for a further twenty minutes or so, an instinct born of experience suggested he was being followed. He looked back and saw two riders just cresting the rising trail between the shoulders of land. One was slim, the other bulky. The sun touched something metallic worn by one, striking a brief gleam from it. Almost certainly it was a lawman's badge.

'That damned skinny deputy and, no doubt, his boss, the marshal,' he growled to his horse.

The distant riders halted, clearly aware that they had been spotted. One flourished what was obviously a carbine and Keever ducked his head over his saddle-horn as the weapon blasted and a shell came screaming within inches of him. He hauled out his Peacemaker and pegged a couple of wild shots back at the pair, then hauled his reins to halt his mount.

'I reckon they aimed to sneak up close enough behind me to backshoot me easily,' he muttered to the animal as he swung out of the saddle. Swiftly, he holstered his Colt and yanked the reins to bring his horse to a kneeling position just as another badly aimed rifle shell *whanged* through the air. He drew his heavy weapon from his scabbard, stripped off its waterproof covering, and lay behind his kneeling roan to use the animal as a breastwork and steady the cumbersome carbine across its back.

He fired a crashing, bellowing shot that went

winging towards the cleft in the humped terrain. The riders were now scooting back over the dip in the trail to get out of sight.

'Sensible men,' commended Keever. 'A Sharps Special buffalo carbine is a sure cure for would-be backshooters and I can put a shot between those two humps of land any time you dare show yourselves. Here's some for good measure.'

He triggered the carbine again, sending the shot plumb between the humps of terrain and causing echoes to clatter over the rangeland. There was no sign of the riders who had plainly retreated in the face of his overwhelming firepower. Grinning, Keever fished in the pocket of his slicker and took out a couple of loose shells to replenish the weapon.

He squinted back at the point where the two men had established themselves but they had plainly retreated.

'I figure that pair will keep well out of the way – at least for a spell,' he commented to the roan as he brought it to its feet. He remounted and rode on, reckoning that he must be well on the TT range by now. Half an hour later, he saw two horsemen approaching along the trail.

On cow ponies. Must be TT wranglers, if all of Tom Cardigan's hands haven't deserted him, he mused and he pressed on along the trail to meet the pair head on.

They came straight ahead purposefully and turned out to be a solidly built man nearing middle-age with a neatly trimmed greying moustache and a younger man, darkly bearded and with a suspicious scowl. They were in range-garb, packing Colt revolvers and the bearded man held an 1875 Winchester. His finger was through the trigger-loop.

The two drew rein in front of Keever and Keever halted his roan.

'You're on TT graze,' said the bearded one without ceremony.

'I know it and it's where I aim to be.'

'Why? We don't know you, mister. Have you business here?' asked the suspicious-eyed bearded man but, before Keever answered, the one with the grey moustache cut in, 'We heard shooting from yonder a while back,' he said.

'That was the marshal and deputy from Arrow Ridge. They followed me out of town.'

'Why? Are you wanted?' asked the bearded man.

'No, but that pair didn't want me to reach the TT and find Tom Cardigan,' Keever replied.

The man with the greying moustache leaned forward in his saddle, frowning. He had a mouth which suggested stubborn determination in a face prematurely lined and weathered by life on these northern ranges. He considered Keever with deeply suspicious eyes.

'I'm Cardigan and this is my foreman, Ted Freed,' he stated. 'What do you want with me and who are you?'

'Will Keever.'

The two riders facing him stiffened and the bearded one tightened his finger on the trigger of his Winchester, a spontaneous reaction to hearing the name of a gunfighter of considerable notoriety.

'*The* Will Keever?' asked Tom Cardigan with the suggestion of a gasp.

'Yes – *the* Will Keever.'

A brief, charged silence hung between them then Ted Freed asked, 'What's the story behind Wallis and Twigg coming after you shooting?'

Keever answered, 'Well, I guess they learned my name and figured your outfit has hired my gun. I know Glandon at the Big Three is stacking his bunkhouse with gunhands and running off homesteaders and that he's out to grab your holdings.'

'That's true. All this country knows about Glandon's big ambitions and his methods,' said Cardigan, still with suspicion in his eyes.

'I had a few words with the nosy deputy but told

him nothing except that I'm not about to join up with the Big Three,' continued Keever. 'I also jawed with an old-timer and got the impression that Glandon holds sway in the town. I figure he owns most of it, including its law officers. I spent the night at the hotel. He probably owns that, too. I didn't sign the register until the last minute when I also asked the clerk for directions to the TT.

'He was the only one to learn my name. I figure that, being Glandon's man, once I left, he hotfooted to the law office with the news that Will Keever is in this country and looking for the TT. So the marshal and that nosy deputy reckoned on a speedy backshooting to get rid of a gunsharp with a reputation, who was on his way to back you.'

Keever paused and gave a sardonic laugh and added, 'That'd put them in good with the mighty Mr Glandon. Well, it didn't work and Will Keever is here, bringing his compliments and a willingness to help out.' He slapped his holstered Peacemaker meaningfully.

Tom Cardigan looked at Keever, half puzzled and half angry.

'Now just a minute, Keever,' he said edgily. 'I admit we're threatened by Glandon and his outfit, but I didn't hire you. Why should you just drift on to my spread this way?'

'I wouldn't say I drifted here: I'd say I was impelled to come,' corrected Keever. 'It has to do with your late wife.'

'My wife?' echoed Tom Cardigan.

'Yes. Thalia, a girl from Kansas. She has her initial in your brand, paired with your own. TT stands for Tom and Thalia. You built this spread together. She died young and is buried in a favourite spot near your house. That's one of the reasons why you'll defend your place to the last, as any man worth his salt would.'

The two TT men stared hard, Tom Cardigan with his eyes wide.

'How do you know all about my wife?' he asked huskily, when he found his voice.

'I have good reason to. She had a face you couldn't easily forget, fit to make any man look hard and long. She had black hair and a small mole, plumb in the middle of her chin. You couldn't find a prettier girl on this mortal earth.'

'Yes.' Cardigan almost whispered the word in emotion-charged astonishment. 'That's right.'

Keever pushed his hand inside his slicker and brought out a small leatherette folder. He walked his horse nearer to Cardigan's and handed the folder to the rancher. Cardigan opened it to find that it protected a tintype photograph of a smiling girl – his wife but younger than when he first met her.

'That's her likeness, isn't it?' asked Keever.

'Yes,' said Tom Cardigan throatily. 'But how do you come to have this?'

'Because Thalia was my sister. I'm your brother-in-law, Mr Cardigan.'

CHAPTER TWO

MENACE OVER THE RANGE

Tom Cardigan was struck momentarily dumb but his foreman frowned suspiciously. 'Just a minute,' he said in a voice that was almost a growl. 'You might have that picture, but your story's hard to swallow. I happen to know Mrs Cardigan's maiden name was Travers, not Keever.'

Will Keever smiled wryly. 'Don't tell me you've existed out here in the West without learning that many a man changes his name from the one he was born with, Mr Freed,' he said levelly. 'Travers is an honoured name in a certain section of Kansas and Jack Travers went to the far West, got into one mess of trouble after another and even drew a stretch in a certain territorial pen. His folks back home knew nothing about that and he figured he should save them the pain and embarrassment. He was particularly anxious about his schoolteacher sister whom he heard had married and settled down in Montana. So, Will Keever came into being. I guess Thalia never knew the real identity of Will Keever, who collected so much notoriety, but I reckon she might have mentioned her brother, Jack, once in a while and wondered what became of him.'

'That's right,' responded Tom Cardigan slowly. 'She often spoke of Jack. They lost touch long ago, but he was always on her mind.'

Ted Freed, still cautiously holding his finger on the trigger of his Winchester, asked, 'Those stories about you being a mighty fast gunfighter and killing Cass Chisnall and the Kloot brothers and the rest, were they all true?'

Keever nodded. 'I can claim to be fast, but I never aimed be a gunfighter. I got involved in the Willow Creek land war over in Wyoming, and found myself up against Chisnall and the Kloots. Chisnall was pure poison and both Kloots were more than half crazy. They all wanted me dead, but I was quicker. Smoking it out with the Kloots was the toughest proposition. It was two against one and I got a bullet in the shoulder out of it. When a man gets tagged as a gunfighter, the tag sticks but there were later years when I did other things, like serving as marshal of Apache Wells, down in Arizona. I reckon the folks there considered me a good lawman. All that's behind me, though. I figured you need me to give a hand in your present troubles. By way of making up for all the things I never did for my sister, you understand.'

Tom Cardigan and his foreman had been staring at Keever half-bewildered and with some suspicion, but now suspicion vanished from their eyes. Cardigan urged his cow-pony a little nearer to Keever's mount and reached out an open hand.

'My God, Will Keever, my brother-in-law!' he breathed, as they shook hand solemnly.

Ted Freed shoved his Winchester into his saddle scabbard and emulated the rancher in moving his pony closer to Keever and extended his hand.

Tom Cardigan jerked his head towards the horizon over which he and his foreman had appeared.

'The house is yonder. Better come on over so we can talk,' he invited. 'How come you've shown up out of nowhere – and right at this time, too?'

'It's all due to two fellows who used to ride for

you: Shannock and Dreves. Remember them?' responded Keever.

'Sure,' said Cardigan as all three spurred their mounts. 'A couple of bright youngsters, but they didn't like the way things were shaping up out this way. They saw a range war coming and wanted to get out. I can't blame them for wanting straightforward cowpunching and a peaceable life. They heard outfits down in the south-west were hiring and figured they'd drift out that way to try their luck. And some more of my crew took off for elsewhere. I'm left with only Ted here and five more hands, all veterans who don't scare easily. They're loyal as all get-out and prepared to stand against Glandon's bunch. But what of Shannock and Dreves?'

'They showed up in Apache Wells where I was marshal, hearing that there was a possibility of being hired by one of the outfits in the region. I got into conversation with them and they told me about how things were up on these ranges.' explained Keever. 'They gave a good account of you and the TT, but saw big trouble brewing and they hadn't signed up for any soldiering.'

'That's right,' nodded Cardigan. 'They were good men and they're missed at the TT, but I wouldn't hold any man to anything he had no heart for.'

'I'd never heard of your outfit, but when one of them said your wife had died and was buried on the spread and then mentioned that her name as Thalia, it was like being hit in the heart,' Keever said. 'I'd lost touch with my family years before, ashamed after my prison stretch, but I'd heard a rumour that my sister had gone north, teaching school, and since you don't meet the name Thalia often, I figured I was hearing news of her, sad though it was. When those two boys told me your wife was a Kansas girl, I was sure of it. I got a full story about Glandon and his doings from them and it was plain you were being herded into a hole by him and you needed help. I owed my sister plenty and, after all, you're my brother-in-law, by God. I figured time was short, so I quit my job and headed this way. I managed to put in a few words for Shannock and Dreves at the Bar Seven-Two, a thriving spread in the Apache Wells country, and they were hired.'

'You mean you aim to throw in with us?' queried Ted Freed, with a hint of suspicion.

'Sure. When I reached this country, I made some enquiries and heard plenty about Glandon and his bunch running off homesteaders. I met a family of them, scared as jack-rabbits and moving out, kit and kaboodle. Seems their place was besieged by Glandon's gunnies and they were forced out. I gather Glandon aims to put all these ranges under the Big Three brand by fair means or foul – mostly foul – though I don't know if he's made any definite move against the TT yet.'

'He hasn't yet, but it's coming,' stated Cardigan grimly. 'He's cat-and-mousing and the threat of trouble has already driven away some of my hands, as I told you. He's taken a squad of hardcases on to his payroll.'

'Like who?'

'Like Blackie Harrigan, Karl Froelich and Slim Trotter.'

'All names I know,' said Keever. 'I never met any of them but I've heard of them – and heard nothing good.'

'Glandon is gathering guns and biding his time,' said his brother-in-law. 'Running off homesteaders is only a start. Ultimately, he's playing for high stakes!'

The trio mounted a slope and Keever saw, some distance down the wide sweep of land below, a ranch headquarters typical of the Montana plains country. There was a log-built house, compact but of solid pioneer appearance and fit to withstand the snows, cutting winds, withering sun and torrential rains. Spread around it were barns, stables, a cookhouse and corrals with horses penned in them. The whole was encompassed within a spacious yard.

'There it is,' said Tom Cardigan. 'The place Thalia and I created and it took pains and sacrifices to do it.' He pointed to a small grove of trees on a ridge some distance from the ranch buildings. 'Thalia is buried up there. It was her favourite spot, with a good view of the rangeland.'

Keever narrowed his eyes and focused on the far ridge with a quiver of emotion stirring in him. A fitting spot, he thought, for the final resting place of the spirited, nature-loving sister with whom he had lost touch so long ago.

He was silent for a spell then told Cardigan, 'Your outfit looks worth fighting for.'

'It is,' said his brother-in-law. 'The whole of the TT range is worth fighting for. This is good cow territory, but it's a sure thing that Glandon isn't interested in it just for cattle-raising in the long run.. There's much talk of the railroad coming this way. Right now, the railroad bosses back East are planning to build the tracks through to the Canadian border and, probably, right into Canada itself. There'll be negotiations for land; for the rights of way for the rails and for townsites alongside the tracks over a wide part of this country. You know the huge fortunes that can be raked in through land deals when railroads are involved.'

Will Keever nodded, it was a familiar story. He'd heard versions it before as the underpinning reasons for range feuds elsewhere: the pioneers and the cattlemen came in first and the financial and railroad moguls appeared in their wake, seeking their land. All too often, foul means were employed, resulting in bloody conflicts.

'Glandon is hell bent on getting his hands on these ranges and turning them over to the big money men,' said Cardigan. 'He tried a business approach first, treating me as if I was a yokel and making derisory offers for my holdings. I turned him down flat. Now, he's mad as hell and he's spoiling for a showdown.'

'So, now you're sitting around, waiting for the powderkeg to explode. What do you aim to do – fort up the headquarters and wait until his hardcases come visiting the way they call on homesteaders?' Keever asked.

'I reckon we'll have to sooner or later – and it could be sooner. Glandon might have already started a big play against us. He's in a strong position, though, with more men and he's well armed if real shooting trouble begins.'

'Seems to me something should be done about

stopping him pretty quick.' said Keever.

'Well, I was despondent about the situation up until a few minutes ago when you showed up, Jack,' said Cardigan, 'but, with you around, I feel the balance in regard to gun-savvy might be kind of evened up.'

'I don't make any claims for myself, but I'll admit to having something of a modest reputation,' said Keever. 'Oh, and keep calling me Will Keever. The name of Jack Travers means nothing around here.'

They reached the yard of the TT's headquarters and two men in wrangler garb emerged from the bunkhouse. Both had the wiry and leathery look of veteran cowpunchers.

'Hank, Larry, this here's Will Keever,' called Tom Cardigan, swinging down from his saddle.

The mouths of both men dropped open. '*The* Will Keever?' they gasped in unison.

'Yes. I'll leave Ted to explain about him,' Cardigan replied. 'Unsaddle these cayuses, and give 'em feed and water. I'll take Will into the house for a chinwag. And tell Chang to rustle up some grub and coffee for us.'

Cardigan and Keever walked towards the house and the rancher said, 'There's a spare room you're welcome to have.'

Keever waved the suggestion away. 'No. I'm throwing in with the crew and I don't want anything that looks like privilege. I'll hump my bedroll into the bunkhouse. That is, if I'm being invited to stay.'

'I'll say you are!' Cardigan almost spluttered. 'If ever an outfit needed a man of Will Keever's calibre, this outfit needs you!'

The interior of the house was neat and spacious, with a large fieldstone fireplace. Keever noted with a slight choking sensation how pictures on the wall and delicate ornaments placed here and there reflected the personality and taste of his dead sister. The atmosphere of the house gave him a sense of belonging and he felt that the TT's fate was his concern. If a fight was coming – as it most surely was – it was one in which he would have a very personal stake.

They divested themselves of their heavy slickers and, just as Tom Cardigan pulled a couple of chairs out from the large dining table, a small Chinese man with a cook's apron over a wrangler's jeans and shirt entered, bearing steaming plates on a tray.

'This here's Chang, the best cook ever to drift up this way and just as a good a cattleman if we let him loose from the cookhouse,' said Cardigan.

'Chang, this is—'

'I know, boss, it's Will Keever. Word of his arrival is buzzing around the place and it reached the peaceful and scholarly fastness of my cookhouse pretty damned quick,' cut in Chang. 'His arrival is like manna in the desert. I heard his fame noised abroad long ago and I reckon he's what this outfit needs.'

'Chang is outspoken,' Cardigan commented. 'He's a reading man. That's why he has such a slick turn of phrase.'

'Coffee coming up in five minutes,' stated Chang inscrutably, making for the door.

After they had eaten, Tom Cardigan broke out a bottle of bourbon and filled two glasses. The pair settled into easy chairs.

'So, how did Clay Glandon become the big man here?' asked Keever.

Cardigan gave an ironic smile. 'It happened almost before anyone noticed it. At first, there were three who bought out the L-Box-Bar spread from old Lew Blanchard who had it when Thalia and I first got started here. Glandon, Elias Todd and Charlie Harris were Yankee carpetbaggers. They kept well out of any fighting for the Northern cause but made money through the crooked opportunities the Civil War offered. Then, with the

South defeated, they moved down there with their carpet bags for the rich pickings from broken up plantations and the ruined land. They prospered through plunder and robbery.'

'I reckon I know their style,' nodded Keever. 'After exhausting the pickings down in Dixie, they came up here to the northern plains where the country was opening up, setting themselves up as respectable ranchers.'

'Not so respectable,' Cardigan answered. 'All three were plumb crooked but Glandon was the craftiest rattler of them all. They changed the name of the outfit to the Big Three to glorify themselves, expanded their holdings and pretty well took control of Arrow Ridge. Then Todd and Harris suddenly disappeared. Glandon said he'd bought them out and they'd retired elsewhere but everyone suspects he got his claws on their money, arranged their deaths and they're likely to be buried somewhere on Big Three land.'

'Riding here, you said Glandon might have started to make his play. How?' asked Keever.

Tom Cardigan reached across and refilled Keever's glass. 'That's something Ted Freed and I had just been investigating when we heard your shooting ruckus out yonder. We have a creek running though our land and it comes down through the Big Three before it reaches us. It's a source of water for our stock and, by all the laws of the range country, both the Big Three and TT have unfettered rights to it. It's essential to the health of our land and cattle, particularly in dry times. Just lately, we've noticed that the creek is beginning to run low and that's plumb peculiar considering the wet spell we've had. If its gets much lower and if a dry spell comes on, it could mean trouble, particularly with the spring roundup coming up. Ted and I had been out to look at the condition of it and it's getting worse—'

Anticipating the trend of his narrative, Keever interrupted, 'And you figure it's the old game of water rustling. The flow of the creek being interfered with up on the Big Three spread – through being dammed, for instance?'

'Sure. That's the only explanation. We've had some deluges of rain lately and to have the creek so low is unnatural.'

Keever drained his glass and pronounced slowly, 'Well, that, by God, is something else that needs attention!'

His glass was replenished by his brother-in-law and they talked further for a long spell during which Keever learned much about both the sister whom he had scarcely known in her later years and the man she married. Though he wanted no material stake in the TT Ranch, it came to him that if, after a wandering, turbulent and rootless life, he had any emotional claim on a place to call home, it was here, on the cattle enterprise into which Thalia and her husband had sunk all their hopes. Here, where Thalia was buried in land she came to love.

Kinship bound him to Tom Cardigan and the TT and the rancher and his spread were under the glowering threat of a range war that might turn out to be as bloody as any so far seen on these restless northern cattlelands.

Heading for the bunkhouse, he reflected again that Tom Cardigan was plainly too law-abiding and too decent to initiate action against Glandon and his outfit. But passive sitting around waiting for the Big Three to force the issue was downright irksome and certainly not the style of Will Keever. In fact, he was beginning to feel a restless and irresistible itch that he knew only too well.

Keever established himself in the bunkhouse, claiming an empty bunk. As he encountered each man of the TT crew, he mentally took his measure and he liked the sum total of the foreman and the small squad of hands who had stuck with the outfit.

In addition to Ted Freed, there were Hank Sands, Larry Thorsen, Shorty Cannon, Mex Cortez and Chang, the scholarly cook.

Their stolid adherence to the TT said much about them and Keever liked the look of them. In time, he would find that his instincts were correct. All were veterans of the frontier and all were imbued with its ethics. None asked too searchingly about the background of his fellows; none among the older members enquired as to which side a man fought on in the War Between the States and no one gave a damn whether a man's father was a pauper or a European duke.

All of these hands had served the TT since its inception with an unswerving loyalty to Tom Cardigan and to the memory of his late wife, Will Keever's sister. This, thought Keever, had the look of a crew fit to ride the river with, as the old Western saying had it.

CHAPTER THREE

MISSION TO ARROW RIDGE

'You mean you had him in your sights and you missed?' bawled Clay Glandon. 'And now Will Keever has hooked up with Tom Cardigan! Will Keever, of all people, on the TT's payroll? How the hell did Cardigan get hold of him? And why the hell did you allow Keever to pass through town? You should have known about him!'

Glandon's roaring almost caused the solid structure of the Big Three ranch house to shudder.

Glandon was a big and hefty man and his current temper was almost as towering as his frame. There was nothing jovial about the plumpness of his face; rather, there was a foxiness to his well-fed visage. He moved with an edginess which suggested a constant, guilty looking over his shoulder. He had nothing of the open, expansive character of the genuine cowman of wide-skied Montana. Though he sought a show of respectability in the black broadcloth suiting favoured by preachers and lawyers, there remained in him much that suggested dubious origins in a seething slum of an eastern city.

His lung power suited his big body and his vaulting ambition and he was now giving Arrow Ridge's lawmen, Wallis and Twigg, the full blast of it.

The pair had hastened to the Big Three headquarters immediately after beating their retreat from the scene of their attempted bushwhacking of Will Keever. Now, they stood shamefaced before the rancher in his well-appointed living-quarters, apprising him of their ill-luck – or as much of it as they dared reveal. Under no circumstances would they admit that Sam Twigg had actually conversed with Keever when he arrived in town without discovering either his identity or his destination.

Marshal Wallis and his deputy were sticking firmly to a yarn that it was not until they heard from the hotel clerk that they knew anything of Keever's presence in Arrow Ridge or that he was

41

bound for the TT Ranch.

So, just when Clay Glandon believed he held all the cards to crush the owner of the TT outfit and could take his sweet time about it, Tom Cardigan appeared to have acquired a hired gun. And he was not just any gunslinger: he was Will Keever, whose reputation stretched from the deserts of the south-west to these high plains, nudging the Canadian border.

'Keever!' shouted Glandon again. 'How the hell did he get Keever? Dammit, I got Slim Trotter and Blackie Harrigan and Karl Froelich and I might have got Keever, too, only there was a story he'd kicked over the traces and taken to badge-carrying. I would have paid him plenty, so how did Cardigan grab him for his payroll? Answer me that.'

But it was beyond the powers of his tame lawmen to do so. Not that they were given much of a chance for Glandon loosed another tirade at them.

'You two might have known he spent the night in town if you had your eyes open. He slipped past you so you took off on a damnfool chase which finished with him sending you running scared,' he snorted.

'It was that buffalo gun of his, Mr Glandon,' faltered Rufe Wallis. 'He damned near hit the pair of us. You can't answer that kind of weapon with Winchesters. A Sharps can nearly blow a man in half.'

'That's right, Mr Glandon,' said skinny Sam Twigg. 'And he had the advantage of higher ground than us.'

'He had the advantage when it came to brains, too,' growled Glandon. 'It's a good thing I have men worth their salt on the Big Three payroll. Having Will Keever siding with Cardigan is a big complication.' He flicked back one side of his broadcloth frock and slapped his hand on the butt of the Navy Colt belted across his ample middle. 'Keever's hash has to be settled pretty damn quick.'

After another lurid broadside at the hapless pair, Glandon snarled, 'Get the hell back to town, you're doing no good hanging around here! Not that you ever do much good in town,' he yelled. 'All you're capable of is loafing and blundering and I'm damned if I'll stand much more of it.'

Wallis and Twigg squirmed in the face of Glandon's raging. They had attempted to ingratiate themselves with him by trying to bushwhack Keever on learning that he was bound for the TT and, on admitting their failure, met with what they expected – the rancher's bellowing wrath.

They were about to scoot out of the room when Clay Glandon halted them with his mouth set in a grim line.

'Will Keever on the TT's payroll can only mean Cardigan is coming out of his hole and fixing for a fight!' he said. 'Well, I have guns enough to meet any fight the TT brings on, but I'll make sure that Cardigan is starved of ammunition. The only place he can get it is at Ike Jilks's store in town. So far, I allowed it because I've played it soft with Cardigan, trying to negotiate with him, but I own the store Jilks is trading out of so you tell Jilks I'll run him out of the place if he sells guns or ammunition to Cardigan and his bunch. I'll close up his business and clear the cantankerous old horned toad out of town as fast as I clear the blasted homesteaders off these ranges. You tell Jilks that and tell him good.'

Arrow Ridge's paunchy chief law officer gulped. 'Yes, Mr Glandon,' he answered feebly. Then he and his deputy departed quickly.

Clay Glandon paced the floor with his twitchy apprehension much in evidence.

'By God, I'll spike Tom Cardigan's guns every whichway,' he muttered to the empty room. 'Not only will I dry up his source of ammunition, I have my ace in the hole already working.'

Briefly, the big rancher's mood brightened and

44

he smirked, contemplating the scheme he had devised to ruin his neighbour and further his avaricious plans, and he growled with relish, 'When I'm through, a dried-out range will knock the guts out of the TT. By roundup time, Cardigan's hands will be gathering worthless hide and bones.'

'It looks pretty damned bad,' said Tom Cardigan angrily. He, Ted Freed, Will Keever and the veteran hand Larry Thorsen, sat on horseback contemplating the creek on the TT range.

It was the morning after Keever's arrival at the TT and the four set out early to assess the state of the creek. They found the water worryingly low. Its level had dropped so severely that the creek was margined by tracts of the muddy bed.

'And we know what's causing it,' growled the TT's foreman. 'There's no doubt about the creek being dammed over on the Big Three's territory. It's a deliberate grab of our water for sure.'

'But the dam must be somewhere close enough to the TT range to ensure it's the TT outfit that suffers,' commented Will Keever. 'A dam too far into his own territory would mean Glandon robs his own range of water.'

'By thunder, this is more serious than I figured,' muttered Cardigan. 'We've put up with plenty, but we can't put up with dried-up range this close to roundup. Glandon's done enough dirty work. He's run off homesteaders, bought up most of Arrow Ridge with his filthy money, got his grasp on the so-called law officers who even tried to bushwhack Will here. He attempted to buy me out with offers of nickels and dimes and now he's rustling my water!'

'We've been taking too much lying down, boss,' said Larry Thorsen with a belligerent scowl. 'We'll have to ante up and fight Glandon.'

'Damn it, Larry's right. This is a plain invitation to start a range war,' muttered Freed. 'We'll have to fight Glandon, boss.'

'We will!' replied Tom Cardigan forcefully. 'We'll lay in supplies of ammunition and, for all his hired gunslicks, we'll take the fight to him!'

'Well, I'm ready, boss,' said Larry Thorsen with enthusiasm. 'And I reckon the rest of the boys are. We've all seen it coming for long enough.'

'We have to think of the logistics of a range war,' said Cardigan calmly. 'The only convenient source of ammunition for both sides is Ike Jilks's gun store in Arrow Ridge. We'll have to move fast and, even so, we might find Glandon has grabbed all his stock already.'

'Then let's move right now,' suggested Keever.

46

'It's still early. We can be in town before the place is properly awake and, if Glandon hasn't beaten us to it, we'll grab whatever stock we can.'

Cardigan said: 'That'd mean we're tipping our hand. I reckon word of our move will get back to Glandon pretty quick.'

'There's no other choice. We just can't afford to be without ammunition with a range-war threatening,' Keever pointed out. 'Anyway, there's no harm in letting Glandon know we're ready for a fight and no one has any right to stop us doing business in Arrow Ridge – not even Clay Glandon. I suggest a party of us goes into town in search of ammunition and we'll see what Mr Glandon makes of it.'

'It'll be risky but, by grab, I like the sound of it,' said Tom Cardigan. 'It'd show Glandon we're not taking his threats lying down.'

They made a hasty return to the TT headquarters where all hands entered into a council of war and each showed willing to participate in the quest for ammunition. Tom Cardigan wanted to lead the action alongside Keever. Ted Freed, as foreman, claimed the right to be his boss's lieutenant. Larry Thorsen and the saturnine and usually silent Mex Cortez, both known as useful gunhands, were selected to back them up.

Their plan was put into action even before

noon, a time by which Arrow Ridge was hardly ever fully awake. The five set off, armed and looking businesslike, Keever, Cardigan and Freed on horseback and Thorsen and Chavez riding a buckboard wagon since the party's aim was a bulk purchase of ammunition.

They took the trail from the ranch house over the folds of the rangeland to where it broadened into a wider ribbon, eventually leading to the town.

Unknown to them, a party of trespassing observers spotted them from a clump of oaks on the crest of a distant rise: four men on sturdy cow ponies, who immediately dismounted and hauled their animals back into the obscurity of the trees while maintaining a sharp watch on the party. One, the burly and loutish foreman of the Big Three, Dan Flagel, had a spyglass trained on the far riders and wagon.

'Five of 'em – Cardigan, Freed, Thorsen, the Mexican and that damned Keever,' he reported. He folded the spyglass quickly, careful not to linger too long with it to his eye, risking the morning sun striking a telltale glint from it. 'Five of 'em, headed for town with a wagon. They're up to something.'

On Glandon's orders, this Big Three party had

taken the risk of venturing on to TT rangeland that morning to ascertain the effects of the dam the Big Three had just completed to deprive Tom Cardigan's outfit of water. Hence Flagel's spyglass.

The farther side of this rise offered a good view of the creek winding over the TT range and they saw with satisfaction that the volume of water was clearly thinned down. The creek was now more a thread than its usual broad stream.

Dan Flagel was accompanied by two unsavoury hands, Jack Kerr and Kid Sisley who had taken part in running off homesteaders with keen enthusiasm. The other rider was Blackie Harrigan, one of the trio of gunhands with reputations augmenting the Big Three payroll. He was with the party for intimidation purposes in case the intruders were intercepted by TT hands. His once jet hair and longhorn moustache were grey these days and Flagel had noticed a tremor in his hand. Privately, the Big Three foreman had doubts about the current validity of Harrigan's reputation. Once, the Big Three's hefty foreman watched him sneak into the shadow of a barn and, thinking he was unobserved, take a substantial pull from a hip-flask.

'Up to something?' said Kid Sisley. 'Maybe we should follow them. Mr Glandon would like to know what they're up to.'

'Maybe we should,' agreed Flagel, 'but, if anything starts, they have Keever with them.'

'So what?' growled Blackie Harrigan disdainfully. 'D'you figure *I* can't take Keever? Don't make any mistake, I can settle Will Keever's hash any time I get the inclination. I have a place on my gun to cut a notch in his memory.'

'It's four of us against five of them,' cautioned Jack Kerr. 'If we follow them, we'd have to be plumb sure they didn't catch sight of us on TT graze.'

'Sure, but in town, we'd have Wallis and Twigg, for what they're worth, to back us,' said Flagel. 'And this TT bunch is surely headed for town.'

The Big Three's foreman knew well enough that Wallis and Twigg were not worth much but the idea of discovering what the TT party was about was beginning to appeal to him. It could be a means of ingratiating himself with Clay Glandon, though he was highly apprehensive about Keever, the trigger-tripper from the south-west with the big reputation. 'We'll follow them in, keeping well out of sight behind them,' he conceded. 'There's something blamed cocksure about the way that bunch is riding. We have to find out what Cardigan's play is. But we'll go cautiously.'

The intruders waited until they saw the TT

riders disappear where the trail swung round a far hillock then rode warily out of the stand of trees, down to the trail and followed at a safe distance.

As the party from the TT neared the town, the air was warming – perhaps with a spring warmth which might belie the recent rains and betoken dryness yet to come. And a dry spring would bode ill for the TT range with the creek running low and the round-up looming.

The party halted and surveyed the higgledy-piggledy settlement. The street had a few people, a stray dog, a couple of hitched horses and a pair of wagons. The recent rain had left puddles and tracts of wheel – and hoof-mauled mud along the street.

From their good vantage point, the TT riders could see the town-marshal's office, with its door closed; then, across the street, the clapboard bulk of the hotel where Keever had spent his first night in the town, likewise devoid of any sign of life.

They took in the restaurant and, a few doors from it, the store bearing the sign: IKE JILKS GUNSMITH – GUNS AND AMMUNITION.

'Everything fine and dandy and the town looks mighty welcoming,' said Keever. 'Let's go in.'

The TT men continued on, angling their course over towards the hitching post outside the gun

51

shop. All looked dead ahead but Keever's tail-of the-eye glance towards Wallis's office revealed a glimpse of the lawman, watching from its narrow window.

Behind the window, Wallis stared slack jawed and he felt a chill. Here was a bunch from the TT, including Cardigan and his foreman, Freed and Will Keever, whom he believed to be Cardigan's hired gunhand, in town, and audaciously heading for the gun and ammunition store forbidden to the TT by Clay Glandon. And only a couple of hours since he and his deputy had dutifully warned Ike Jilks that no weapons or ammunition must be sold to the TT outfit.

Jilks, noted for his crossgrained attitude to life, met threats of being hounded out of Arrow Ridge by merely grunting that he was in business to deal with any customer he chose to and it was no damned business of Glandon or the town's law officers. Rufe Wallis figured there'd be trouble with Jilks, and now this TT bunch was drawing up at the gun store, bringing a buckboard.

Deputy Sam Twigg, attracted by his superior's intent stance before the window, came behind Wallis and watched with equal discomfort, interpreting the signs for himself. After the rough handling endured by the pair, this placed the lawmen in a hole. The self-appointed ruler of Arrow Ridge would expect Wallis and his deputy to do something about this development – in the form of decisive action.

The lawman watched the TT riders reach the gun shop. Three, Cardigan, his foreman and Keever descended from their saddles and hitched their reins. Thorsen and Cortez came down from the wagon and the whole party mounted the plankwalk and entered the store. Keever had unshipped his buffalo carbine from its scabbard and he carried it with him.

Rufe Wallis considered the situation with fear and apprehension. He was plain scared of Keever, with his big reputation and the high calibre weapon he favoured and he almost quaked in his boots at the thought of Keever seeking retribution for the failed bushwhacking attempt. Of the others in the party, the marshal knew that Thorsen and Cortez in particular had always showed themselves peaceable, but there were tales around these ranges that they had gun-savvy and had figured in some wild exploits in days gone by. Wallis wished the scene unfolding before his eyes was not happening.

Inside the gun store, there was a long counter behind which several display cases showed a variety of hand weapons and carbines of various makes. There were also shelves of boxed ammunition but it was plain that the store was not greatly over-stocked. Keever, remembering his glimpse of the watching marshal, planted himself against the counter and faced the street door with the Sharps Special slanted across his middle and his finger in the trigger loop.

A slightly built, middle-aged and balding man in a check shirt emerged from a door at the further end of the shop. He halted on recognizing Tom Cardigan and the TT hands.

'What can I do for you?' asked the storekeeper in a flat voice.

'Just a modest amount of ammunition, Ike,' said Tom Cardigan.

Ike Jilks raised an eyebrow and said in his unemotional way, 'Well, this is a plumb unusual day for business, Mr Cardigan. Would you believe that, not an hour ago, I had this town's upstanding limbs of the law – both of 'em – in here, telling me that if I so much as sell a slug to your outfit, I'll be run off to hell with my coat tails afire. By order of—'

'—Clay Glandon, King of Arrow Ridge and of all Montana if he has his chance,' finished Tom Cardigan. 'Does that mean we can't do business, Ike?'

Jilks treated his visitors to one of his rare smiles, and stated in his colourless way, 'It sure as hell does not. It's generally considered that Ike Jilks can be pretty blamed cussed. And, right now, I'm just cussed enough to buck Glandon, who has no right to dictate to me who buys or sells here or anywhere else. My dander is up and, if I read the signs aright, at last the TT is standing up to Glandon and the Big Three.'

'You've hit it,' confirmed the rancher.

Jilks's smile broadened. 'Well, I've waited a hell of a time to hear something like that,' he enthused. 'Sure, you can have everything you need. I'll even give you a bonus in the way of some extra shells for that carbine your friend Mr Keever totes, though those weapons are getting to be pretty well obsolete now. I'll do an extra special deal with you; you can have my whole blamed stock for nothing with one condition attached.'

Taken aback, the TT men stared at him and Cardigan asked, 'What's the condition?'

'That you take me with you along with my stock. If you're out to stand against Glandon, I want to be with you,' was Ike Jilks's surprising answer. 'I'm sick of being shoved around and, anyway, my business is running down because this damned town has gone to hell through Glandon. There are no homesteaders left to buy guns and cartridges to hunt for the pot. Of the cow outfits in the territory, there's only you and Glandon to sell to, and this morning he tried to cut you out. I'm damned if I'll wind up supplying only Glandon's outfit out of fear of being kicked out of this place which Glandon owns. Other storekeepers might knuckle down to him, but not me. And certainly not now with signs of a fight coming from you TT men.'

Leaning against the counter, keenly watching the street through the store window, Will Keever grinned. 'Looks like we're getting the bargain of the century, Mr Jilks – a buckboard full of guns and ammunition and our own gunsmith to boot and all for free. '

Larry Thorsen, still bewildered, said, 'I never took you for a fighting man, Ike, but I reckon the TT needs you. I figured you'd be pretty wary of Glandon if not plumb scared of him like the rest of the storekeepers.'

'I lay low and took a lot from Glandon, but it's high time I let fly with my real feelings,' said Jilks. 'I'll take him on. I have no kith or kin to be intimidated and, as for not being a fighting man, try me. I learned some rough stuff long ago and far away from here. I can teach Clay Glandon a trick or two.'

The gun dealer dropped his voice dramatically, then continued, 'I never told it too loud because there are still old Union Army men around who'd like to get even with me, but I was with Mosby's Raiders during the big war. And now that I see a battle on the horizon, blamed if the old Rebel spirit isn't stirring in me. They'll tell you Ike Jilks is pretty damned ornery; well, right now, I'm ornery enough to help you load up your wagon right in the face of Glandon's lawmen and hit the trail for trouble along with you.'

'With Mosby – you?' said Tom Cardigan unbelievingly. The short, hardly heroic- looking Ike Jilks scarcely gave the appearance of one who had ridden with John Singleton Mosby's Confederate Raiders in the Civil War. The audacious and daring exploits of Mosby's men had already passed into legend. Even the usually silent Mex Cortez was moved to comment on this news.

'Mosby? He was a plenty powerful *bandido*, I think,' he observed.

'*Bandido* be damned,' snorted Jilks. 'He was a soldier. All Mosby's men were soldiers, but just a little unorthodox and I'm not too old to be still infected by the old Mosby spirit. What do you say, Mr Cardigan? Do we have a bargain?'

'We do,' affirmed Tom Cardigan energetically.

'Let's get to loading the wagon.'

Helped by Ike Jilks, whose old rebel spirit was making him eager for a fight, the TT party began to clear his shelves with gusto, hardly able to believe their good fortune.

But they had yet to get safely out of Arrow Ridge with their valuable cargo of the materials of war.

CHAPTER FOUR

CLASHING GUNFIGHTERS

Dan Flagel and the other Big Three riders were growing good and sick of Mackie Harrigan's big talk. They were close to town and Harrigan had been talking up his intention of putting paid to the threat posed to the Big Three by Will Keever's presence on the TT's strength.

The brutish Flagel had a short temper at the best of times and an extended trail journey listening to Harrigan's mouthing his deadly intentions towards Keever was proving extremely irksome. His companions felt the same way though they had some fear of Harrigan because of the reputation he had built up in the past. Flagel was wary of him, but, having for the first time been thrust into his company as a trail companion, it was rapidly fading. Harrigan was full of war talk directed at Will Keever, but Flagel interpreted his obvious edginess as fear of the man from the south-west. He felt Harrigan was talking to boost his own courage.

Will Keever was exercising other minds at that very moment, namely those of Marshal Rufe Wallis and Deputy Sam Twigg.

Still watching from the window of their office, the eyes of the pair were riveted on the scene across the sheet. They saw the party from the TT, accompanied by Ike Jilks, troop out of the gun store with their arms laden with weapons and wooden ammunition boxes which they loaded into the buckboard. They then returned to the store for further loads.

Keever, who by now had ceased anticipating any trouble from the town's lawmen, jammed his Sharps Special into the saddle-boot of his tethered horse and joined the others in making several journeys in and out of the store to load the wagon.

'By grab, they'd emptying the blasted store! Taking every last gun in the place and all of the ammunition by the look of it – and right after we warned Jilks about doing any business with the TT!' spluttered Wallis.

'And Jilks is with 'em. He's helping 'em load up,' Twigg said unbelievingly. 'We'll have to do something about it.'

Rufe Wallis gulped. 'I'm playing it cautiously,' he jittered. 'There's only two of us and there's a bunch of them. I'm not rushing out bald-headed to face Thorsen and Cortez; they both know how to shoot and that damned Keever is too much of a challenge. He's sure to be gunning for us, remember. I don't aim to go out without some thought first.' The marshal drew his pistol as if it was a decisive gesture. Privately, Sam Twigg considered that his superior had no intention of going out at all.

Dan Flagel and his companions appeared at the head of the street and were only just visible from the window of the marshal's office. Wallis and Twigg watched them rein up and look down the street, obviously taking in the scene outside the gun store.

Their arrival put some spirit into Sam Twigg. 'Here's Flagel with Harrigan, Kerr and Sisley,' he said. 'They'll back us. There'll be six of us and five of the TT crew. Mr Glandon will expect us to do something and the odds are with us.'

'They're not,' countered Wallis. 'Harrigan is the

only real gunhand with them.' Sisley and Kerr and Flage are nothing special.' It was the plain truth. Flagel, Sisley and Kerr were bullies, good for nothing but scaring harmless homesteaders with threats and wild shooting.

'I'm giving it some thought,' said Wallis.

Out on the street, the riders from the Big Three began to walk their horses slowly towards the TT men and their buckboard. As if by responding to some unseen telegraphic message, groups of Arrow Ridge citizenry were gathering and standing around in anticipation of some drama unfolding before their eyes.

'There's trouble on the way!' called Ted Freed, who was the first to spot the approaching Big Three horsemen. The TT party at the buckboard immediately stopped loading the vehicle and formed a defensive cluster. They waited, watching the rival group pace their mounts towards them and tension climbed with the party poised to grab their side arms.

The newcomers rode ahead but with marked caution. 'Well, how about that for nerve?' gasped Dan Flagel. 'Looks like they're taking everything in Jilks's shop. And that damned Keever is with them. They're arming themselves to make a full-scale fight. The TT has sure got gutsy since Keever showed up. Better play things easy. His Sharps is in his saddle scabbard and his horse is hitched but he could still make a grab for that damned carbine. He needs watching.'

'Keever be damned!' snorted Harrigan. 'I can take him any time. I could even if he had his blasted buffalo gun in his fists.'

'So, go ahead. Ante up!' said Dan Flagel tauntingly. 'Do the stuff Mr Glandon took you on the payroll for.'

Blackie Harrigan, stung by the foreman's provocative attitude and seeing now that he had talked himself into a hole, growled, 'I'll ante up all right.'

He boldly urged his mount forward ahead of his hesitant companions. There were, however, icy qualms in his guts. It was a long time since he last flourished his gun in one of the flamboyant cowtown smoke-outs that had given him a reputation. The truth was that his great days were in the past him and he knew it. He held his place at the Big Three on tattered credentials, but after his windy war talk on the trail, he knew he had to make good on his boasting.

He spurred his mount slightly to quicken it towards the TT party at the buckboard. Keever watched his approach with a wooden expression.

The Big Three horsemen reined and drew their animals back and the knot of Arrow Ridge townsfolk likewise drifted further away as the distance between the slowly advancing horseman and the group at the buckboard dwindled.

Will Keever had never seen Harrigan before but he guessed the identity of the rider with his full, greying moustache which had probably once been black.

Keever moved towards the centre of the street and spread his legs and, in front of the approaching rider, held a stance which suggested stubborn immovability. He kept his right hand well away from his holstered Peacemaker Colt.

Harrigan halted his animal only yards from him. And shouted, 'I'm calling you, Keever! You're causing mischief and Mr Glandon doesn't like mischief in his town.'

'And I suppose you're some concerned citizen who's going to keep order on his behalf, Mr Whoever-You-Are, and you aim to stop me,' responded Keever.

'Sure, I aim to stop you,' Harrigan called. 'And you know damned well who I am.'

'I figure you must be Blackie Harrigan,' replied Keever. 'I heard a lot about you years ago. They said you were a gunfighter to be reckoned with in those days, but you don't look like much now. You got yourself a soft bed in Glandon's bunkhouse and his greenbacks in your poke, but I wouldn't say he got himself much of a bargain.'

'You've got a hell of a big mouth, Keever,' snarled Blackie Harrigan.

'I can back anything that comes out of it any time you're ready to make your play,' Keever called calmly.

'I'll make it – if I can get out of my saddle without being gut-shot by you while I'm occupied in doing it,' said Harrigan. He was now feeling with some surprise that his qualms were clearing. He was beginning to experience a revival of the old challenge of combat he knew in the roaring frontier towns of earlier years.

'I shoot fair and square, Harrigan. I'll draw when you have both feet on the ground and are facing me with an equal chance,' Keever told him.

There was another alarmed scooting back of Arrow Ridge citizenry as Blackie Harrigan came down from his horse and faced Keever. Like Keever, he adopted a spread-legged gunfighter's stance and a dramatic tension hung between the pair.

'I'm shutting your mouth for keeps, Keever,' spat Harrigan. His right hand grabbed for his holstered Colt and cleared it from leather with dazzling speed which proved that his pistol prowess had far from gone to seed.

The watchers on the street never saw Will Keever's right hand move for his holster but it was suddenly full of a Peacemaker that barked a single echoing blast toward Harrigan.

Harrigan abruptly jerked bolt upright and, with a crimson splotch spreading on his chest, fell forward through a drifting scarf of gunsmoke. His gun, directed at Keever, was slanted upwards at a sharp angle and, before he hit the ground, some dying spasm caused his finger to trip the trigger.

The weapon exploded at point-blank range and the watchers saw Keever lurch to one side as if poleaxed.

Keever felt a stunning impact at his left temple and his last fleeting, fractured thought before total blackness swallowed him, was that he had entirely misjudged Blackie Harrigan's potential as a killer. He staggered then fell and lay still in the rutted dirt.

'Hell – Keever and Harrigan have killed each other!' exclaimed Sam Twigg, hoarsely.

The skinny deputy, with his nose almost pressed against the office window, was transfixed by the drama out on the street. Beside him, big Marshal Rufe Wallis was all but frozen with horror.

They saw the TT men around the laden buckboard hold still for a brief spell, then they began to act. Thorsen and Cortez swiftly drew their revolvers. Tom Cardigan and Ike Jilks ran to the still form of Will Keever, grabbed his shoulders and hauled him back to the wagon with his spurs trailing in the beaten dirt of the street. They lifted him and lay him on the cargo of ammunition boxes, carbines and pistols.

Glandon's tame law officers could not hear what was being said by the TT group, but Cardigan appeared to be giving orders. They saw his foreman, Ted Freed, unhitch his own horse and those of Cardigan and Keever from the rack outside the gun store.

Acting speedily, Cardigan and Freed swung into their saddles and Freed handed the reins of Keever's roan to Ike Jilks after Jilks had finished putting Keever into the wagon. Thorsen and Cortez climbed into the seat of the buckboard. Passing his Colt to Mex Cortez, Larry Thorsen took the reins while Cortez, now armed with two hand weapons, held both menacingly in the direction of Dan Flagel and his pair of Big Three companions, mounted only a short distance ahead of the gun store and positioned at the edge of the street. They held still poses and made no move for their guns.

To make their retreat, the TT party needed to pass Flagel, Kerr and Sisley. Although outnumbered, the Big Three group might still make trouble, having some advantage from the fact that the TT men were encumbered by a heavily laden wagon. But still Flagel, Kerr and Sisley sat their horses with their weapons holstered. They seemed to be hypnotized by the corpse of Blackie Harrigan, sprawled in the middle of the street while his horse stood nervously kicking at the dirt.

The numbers of watching citizens had swelled, more having arrived attracted by the sound of the shooting. They held themselves back at a safe distance and witnessed the TT party spur their horses and set the buckboard rumbling forward, making as much speed as possible.

Approaching the mounted Big Three men, Mex Cortez on the wagon's seat, swung the mouths of his two Colts towards then and Tom Cardigan and Ted Freed had them covered from their saddles.

Dan Flagel lacked the guts to push any gunplay, but he was at last moved to make some token gesture of defiance.

'You won't get away with this, Cardigan!' he

bawled. 'You figure you're fixing for a war, and you'll get it. Mr Glandon will be settling his bill with you. You've grabbed yourself a real tiger by the tail!'

'Let him bring it on!' challenged Tom Cardigan. A raging fury at seeing his newly found brother-in-law felled by Blackie Harrigan boiled within him. His instincts had always been peaceable but now he wanted vengeance. 'Tell him to bring it on. We'll be ready for him!'

From the seat of the wagon, Mex Cortez turned his impassive gaze towards Flagel's wide-brimmed hat, squinted at it then fired a well-aimed shot at it to send it spinning from the big man's head.

The TT riders and the wagon passed Glandon's men, making for the end of the street and they hit the homeward trail without the Big Three men taking any action. Their thoughts were on Clay Glandon's reaction to their arrival at the ranch with the corpse of Blackie Harrigan. They took some comfort from the knowledge that the TT men also had a gunfighter's corpse on their hands and the threat posed by Will Keever, the big-name trigger-tripper, was over.

Meanwhile, in the town-marshal's office, Wallis and Twigg still stood immobile at the window.

'There'll be hell to pay for this,' breathed Sam

Twigg. 'What're we going to do about it?'

Marshal Rufe Wallis suddenly came out of his frozen state and appeared to be actually quaking in his boots. He shoved his six-shooter back into its holster and stepped back from the window. 'I know damned well what I'm doing about it,' he stated, showing determination for the first time. 'I'm getting out the back way and making for my cayuse in the stable before Dan Flagel comes over here, poking his nose in.'

Twigg blinked. 'What do you mean?' he asked.

'What do you think I mean, you dimwit? Hell, two killings on the street, one of 'em Glandon's hired gun, and Cardigan's outfit making off with arms and ammunition and with Jilks as well when Glandon told us to make sure they didn't get even a lead slug and you and me did nothing about any of it. Do you think I'm hanging around to face Glandon after this?' He moved towards his desk, unpinned his star, tossed it on the desk then made for the rear door of the office. Before leaving, he turned and called back to Twiggg, 'It should be plain enough what I'm doing. And if you have any brains you'll do the same!'

CHAPTER FIVE

TIGER BY THE TAIL

With the wheels of the buckboard rumbling and the ringbits of the saddle horses jingling, the TT party made good time to the open trail without any pursuit by Dan Flagel and his companions.

On the seat of the wagon, Larry Thorsen handled the reins with Mex Cortez beside him. Tom Cardigan and Ted Freed rode side by side at the head of the vehicle and Jilks, in the saddle of Will Keever's roan, rode to the rear of the buckboard in which Will Keever lay lifelessly on his back on top of the cargo of arms and ammunition. Blood made a crimson splash at his left temple and streaked down the side of his face.

Just as the party slackened pace on reaching a rise in the trail, Jilks suddenly gave a sharp cry, 'Hey, stop the wagon! Keever isn't dead! He's moving!'

In unison, the party drew rein and hastily came down from their saddles. Ike Jilks, nearest to the rear of the wagon, climbed into it quickly. Will Keever's body twitched convulsively for a brief spell, then he struggled to sit up, shaking his head.

The party clustered around the wagon as Jilks steadied Keever and helped him to sit up on one of the boxes of ammunition. Keever looked around bewilderedly.

'Hell! He wasn't killed. Looks like he was just stunned,' exclaimed Tom Cardigan. 'None of us had time to examine him what with all the ruckus back in town.'

Ted Freed joined Ike Jilks in the wagon. He removed Keever's hat which had remained on his head. He looked critically at the wound, then spotted a darkening bruise on Keever's other temple.

'I reckon I know what happened,' he reported. 'Harrigan got off a freak shot just as he fell when Will plugged him. Will was hit on the side of the head, but this isn't a real bullet wound. It's just a graze. The impact knocked him off his feet and he seems to have struck the other side of his head on the ground as he fell. He wasn't killed – just stunned, all right.'

'What the Sam Hill happened?' demanded Keever hoarsely, as his head and his vision cleared. 'And what happened to Harrigan?'

'Mr Harrigan has been elected,' said Jilks, the old Mosby raider, using the Civil War euphemism for loss of life.

Cardigan, visibly relieved, also climbed up into the wagon.

'Damn it, Will. I figured I was going to bury a brother-in-law almost as soon as I became acquainted with him,' he breathed.

Keever slowly came fully to his senses. 'Harrigan was faster than I figured,' he said. 'Right before the shooting started, I was feeling guilty for going up against a guy I thought was old and past his best.'

'He pushed for it, Will. He shot off his mouth about aiming to kill you,' Cardigan reminded him. He removed his bandanna from around his neck and used it to wipe away the streaks of blood on Keever's face. 'He wasn't easy pickings and Clay Glandon still has Karl Froelich and Slim Trotter, both of 'em younger than Harrigan and supposedly plenty dangerous. He has a big crew, too, and every one pretty poisonous. He'll be roaring mad after what you did to Harrigan and after we collected darned near all the arms and ammunition in Arrow Ridge, thanks to Jilks here. I reckon Flagel was right when he said we had a tiger by the tail. We can expect Glandon to come out fighting. Meantime, we have to get back to the TT fast and clean up your wound properly.'

'And prepare for real trouble,' stated Keever gravely.

He came down from the buckboard and mounted his roan while Ike Jilks became a passenger in the wagon and the party pushed on along the n trail. Uppermost in the mind of each of them was the question of how soon Glandon and the Big Three bunch would come looking for retribution.

Back at the ranch house with Keever's head bandaged, Tom Cardigan called all hands together around the cookhouse table for grub and a discussion of strategy in the face of the anticipated threat. The TT had inferior manpower to the Big Three but it was at least bristling with arms thanks to Jilks's surprising action in decamping with the stock of his store. Mention of this fact brought a disgruntled reaction from Chang, the cook.

'Ammunition!' he growled. 'Everyone's rejoicing at our stock of ammunition but, blast it, there's more ammunition than grub on the premises. We'll probably get ourselves into a big war and you fellows will expect me to feed you with what grub we have and it'll be damned hard to get fresh supplies. Why didn't someone think about stock-piling grub as well as ammunition? I'm getting the hell out of here if the grub runs out and any of you look like you're turning cannibal. I never knew an outfit yet where the hands didn't turn on the cook when the going got rough.'

Tom Cardigan was concentrating on plans for the ranch's defences. 'We can expect them to come visiting in force,' he emphasized. 'We'll have to keep a close watch on the place with men posted at our most vulnerable points and with a couple on the roof of the house since it's our highest point and anyone approaching can be spotted from there early.'

'And ammunition stored where everyone can reach it and everyone must know where that is,' put in Keever. 'I suggest we have as many loaded weapons as possible placed ready to hand.'

'We must think of the horses, too,' said Cardigan thoughtfully. 'Raiders will sure as hell try to run them off. We'll have to get them all into the big corral close to the house because it can be defended from the windows.'

Plans unfolded as suggestions came from the hands. The ranch crew went around the interior of the house, shoving furniture and whatever else could form barricades and breastworks against the windows. They quickly loaded pistols and carbines from their ample supply of armaments and placed reserves of weapons within easy reach of the fortified windows.

Ike Jilks drew Will Keever to one side.

'I've been thinking about that dam I heard mention of,' he said confidentially. 'It needs blowing to hell and gone, or, if Tom does save his range, it'll be badly dried out before round-up. I figure there's a way of doing it.'

'You do?' asked Keever, raising an eyebrow.

'Sure. Chang's squawking about having more ammunition than grub around the place made me think about something we once did with Mosby's outfit in the big war. We gave the Yankees a few handfuls of hell just by using a box of black powder cartridges and we brought plenty of those with us when I upped stakes from the store.'

'Tell me more,' urged Keever.

Ike Jilks grinned, as if relishing the memory. 'Well, we had to find a way to put a Union guard post out of action. It was in a plumb inconvenient position, covering a road through which our army

wanted to push troops. There were hardly a handful of Union men in there but the real danger was
the telegraph they'd installed in the post. Our
main force was well out of sight, but that telegraph
could have warned the main body of Yankees of
our force's intentions if the bluebellies in the post
got wind of any Confederate presence near the
road. We were scouting around under Mosby on a
night as dark as the inside of the devil's hat and we
knew we had to blow up that post. The usual way
was to use kegs of gunpowder, but we hadn't any
and dynamite wasn't yet invented, you'll remember. But Mosby always had ideas and we had plenty
of black powder cartridges.'

'You used them to cause an explosion?' queried
Keever.

'Sure thing. Introduce a box of black powder
cartridges to fire and you'll get a plenty big explosion, provided the fire has time to burn into the
box,' grinned Jilks. 'A party of us – me included –
sneaked off on foot into the night with a box of
cartridges. We got right up against the post on its
blind side. We could even hear the Yankees talking
inside. We planted the box against the wall with a
fire under it. We disguised it with rocks as best we
could, then scooted back into the dark and waited.
It blew up all right. The telegraph was put out of

action and the Yankees were caught napping when a swarm of fighting mad Confederates came down that road.'

Keever gave a low whistle. 'You mean we could do the same thing with that dam?' asked Keever.

'Sure, if we can sneak out in the dark and make it to Big Three land without getting caught. It could be that Glandon has the dam guarded and maybe we'll be asking for trouble but, by cracky, I reckon we should try it!'

'I like the sound of it, but we can't spare a squad of men to risk a trip on to Big Three graze with things shaping up the way they are here,' said Keever.

'It should just take two or three – along with that big buffalo carbine of yours,' Jilks said. 'That gun is already talked about around Arrow Ridge and just the sight of it is likely to put a scare into any Big Three jokers guarding the dam.'

Keever considered the plan unfolded by Jilks, who was obviously eager to recapture the piquancy of the risky but exhilarating time when he rode with Mosby's Southern Raiders in the Civil War. Then he thought of the brooding night outside, from which the Big Three might at any moment attack, and doubts emerged.

'We don't know how many men Glandon has

prowling around out there. He might already have some on our graze and we'll be in danger on his land for sure,' he said. 'If we chance it, we'll have to do it tonight, with a small party, acting quickly.'

When it was put to him, Tom Cardigan was immediately attracted by the idea of releasing the water 'rustled' by the Big Three but cautious.

At length, he consented. 'You could be riding right into the teeth of trouble, but it'll be worth a try, so long as there's a chance of your getting back here in one piece,' he declared. 'Remember, you can't be spared.'

'We'll do it,' said Jilks with the eagerness of a schoolboy. 'We'll do it the way I learned from Mosby – in at top speed, hit the enemy, then out at top speed!'

Preparations went ahead. One of Jilks's ample wooden boxes of black powder cartridges was opened, packed tight with an additional number of cartridges and the whole contents smothered in wood shavings soaked in lamp oil, which was also liberally splashed on the outer wooden casing.

'She'll burn like a hayrick once the fire takes, then the whole kit and kaboodle will go up like a volcano,' enthused Ike Jilks.

The party of raiders was chosen from the group that had already distinguished itself in the confrontation in Arrow Ridge: Keever, with his hat pulled well down to cover the giveaway whiteness of his bandage, the trigger-skilled Mex Cortez, the pugnacious Larry Thorsen and Ike Jilks who was positively raring to recapture his wartime spirit.

'Work fast,' urged Tom Cardigan, as they equipped themselves. 'We're too short on manpower to spare you for long.'

The four set off into the darkness, riding towards the Big Three's land, conscious that there might already be hostile intruders on the TT range. They forced their horses to make the best speed possible in the darkness of the moonless night which made landmarks difficult to see.

Back at the house, Cardigan and Ted Freed deployed the small remaining fighting force around the fortified windows. A lookout watched the dark land from the roof and the remuda of horses was penned in the big corral in the yard, within view of the windows. The defenders waited but there was only silence out on the range.

Darkness charged with menace had now fully gathered the folds of grazing, the far rise of hills, the cottonwoods and the pointed pines to itself and, penetrating it, the cautiously travelling dam-raiders reached the creek with its reduced stream and followed its course. The experienced TT men,

Thorsen and Cortez, made a fair guess at where they had crossed from Cardigan's land to that of Glandon's outfit. In open range tradition, the boundary was unmarked for not even Glandon had resorted to sectioning off his holdings with the recently devised barbed wire, an abomination to Montana cattlemen.

A short distance into Big Three land, an upward slant of terrain presented itself and, by straining their eyes from its crest, the riders could faintly make out a dark structure stretched across the creek to block its flow.

'That's it – the dam!' whispered Larry Thorsen.

'Steady,' warned Keever. 'Could be a guard planted on it. Let's hobble the horses and work fast.'

The animals were left on the downward side of the slope within yards of the dam and Thorsen and Cortez carried the bulky ammunition box between them. Keever and Jilks came behind with drawn Colts, with Jilks remembering the way a similar operation was carried out against his wartime enemies.

'Find a dry spot in the dam and make sure the fire is well alight,' he whispered. 'If the box doesn't catch fire, everything is sunk.'

As expected, the dam proved to be made of the

materials found immediately to hand: boulders, large rocks and sections of timber. There were occasional openings in it allowing an amount of water to flow through to the sectioned off creek bed and on into TT land.

'They needed to ease some pressure or they'd flood the surrounding Big Three land. I reckon they've built some kind of temporary reservoir back yonder to hold what they're rustling from TT graze,' muttered Jilks.

Will Keever nodded. 'And Glandon probably has ideas of building a more permanent reservoir. It sure makes a choice proposition for a railroad depot and townsite if he manages to grab TT land to add to his own – a sweet little spot with a water system already tamed and ripe for development.'

They worked as rapidly as the dark night permitted and found a dry location away from any of the gaps allowing the restricted escape of water, scrabbling around, seeking rocks to be piled around the ammunition box in the form of a crude fireplace. This was filled with oil-soaked wood-shavings which they had brought in a warsack.

'Just like the old days when I was with Mosby,' said Jilks, grinning in the darkness. 'All we need now is the good luck we had then.'

He sparked a wheel-and-flint lighter into action

and touched its flame to the oil-sodden material around the box and it began to burn rapidly. Satisfied with its progress, the four scooted back to their animals on the nearby rise.

They grabbed their reins, pulled the horses down to the kneeling position and crouched beside them with drawn guns. Keever, having unshipped his Sharps, knelt on one knee with the intimidating weapon ready.

They waited, watching the fire in its nest of rocks against the dam wall, flickering dimly from this distance. At the same time, they kept wary eyes on the darkness beyond the shadowy bulk of the dam. Suddenly, the faraway whinnying of a horse came on the slight spring breeze. Then another, thinned by distance but plainly audible.

The TT men turned their gaze to the direction of the sound but saw only blackness.

'There's more than one, somewhere along the bank of the creek back there in the darkness,' whispered Keever. 'Maybe they're mounted, or maybe they're camped with their horses picketed.'

'Or maybe they're on the move and coming this way,' murmured Mex Cortez. He dropped to his knees and put his ear to the ground, Indian fashion. 'Moving,' he reported. 'Slowly, but moving this way. Probably, they're patrolling the bank of the creek. Two, but maybe three horses, reckon.'

The four crouched in the darkness, clutching the reins of their kneeling animals. Breathless and anxious, they continued their watch on the faint flicker only just visible over by the wall of the dam where they had set the fire.

It seemed to take an eternity for any sign of a decisive development and each of the four had his private fear that the flames would simply die before the oil-soaked wooden cartridge box caught fire.

Out in the darkness to one side of the dam's position, a flame flared as someone lit a smoke, then came the sound of plodding horses, then the jingle of ringbits and, eventually, a dull buzz of conversation between a couple of unseen riders.

'They're coming this way,' reported Thorsen.

Instinctively, three of the TT men lifted their Colts while Keever curled his finger around the trigger of the Sharps Special.

The sound of the riders approaching out of the blackness, grew louder. Then one of the unseen mounts gave a sudden whinny, obviously responding to the nearness of the animals of the TT men.

Mex Cortez's horse treacherously answered with a long, quivering whinny.

'Hell, there's someone there!' yelled a hoarse

and urgent voice. Then, it added in alarm, 'And look – there's a fire, right there against the dam!'

At that same instant, the wooden ammunition box over at the dam caught fire, spreading a sudden splash of light over the immediate scene.

In the flash of illumination, the four TT men saw two riders, only yards away and with sixguns drawn. Both were recognizable as Big Three wranglers, leaning forward in their saddles and staring wide-eyed at the intruders.

Keever, Jilks, Cortez and Thorsen stood up, flourishing their guns. In the abrupt flaring of the firelight, Keever was to the fore, a menacing apparition – to the Big Three men, the wraith of a gunfighter with his huge carbine at the ready and only a matter of mere yards in front of them.

'*Cardigan's men! And Keever's ghost with that damned big gun!*' screeched one almost hysterically. '*Get back, quick!*'

Panicking, he hauled his reins to wheel his horse, and his companion also drew his animal back hastily. In the quickly fading flare of light, the men from the TT saw the two slither their mounts back down the slope and nearer to the structure of rocks and logs which held back the bulk of the creek's volume.

In wild haste, one loosed a shot and a bullet

went screaming past the TT men. Then, a split second later, the box of black powder cartridges at the base of the dam blew up with a deafening, shuddering blast.

Its force slammed into Keever and his companions, almost knocking them off their feet. Shattered timber and rock was forced up into the air then the released water deluged out of the breach in the dam wall. Crouching on the slanted land, ducking low and trying to control their panicky horses, the TT men heard an indistinct mingling of hoarse yells of alarm and screeching animals as, down by the dam now shrouded by the night again, the pair from the Big Three were overwhelmed by the power of the water surging out of the broken dam into the deprived creek bed.

Oddments of rock and shards of timber were falling around the TT party as they gasped for breath, holstered their weapons and fought to control their animals.

They mounted up and instinctively spurred horseflesh to beat a retreat.

Audible evidence of struggling men and horses, floundering in the released water, sounded from behind them as they pounded away.

'Anyone hurt?' shouted Keever.

'A rock hit my hat – nearly brained me,' panted Jilks.

'Something nicked my ear,' complained Mex Cortez.

'And I lost my hat,' growled Larry Thorsen.

It seemed, however, that the four and their animals were positioned on the very fringe of the force of the explosion and so were only slightly affected, where Glandon's men, having retreated nearer the creek bed and much closer to the dam, had taken its full force and that of the violently released volume of water.

Keever had managed to slide his carbine back into its scabbard even while grappling with his frightened roan and, so far as he was aware, he and his mount were in no way injured.

The four split the night breeze, urging their animals up the rising land, then down to follow a creek bed rapidly filling with a surge of water resembling a tidal wave and on to TT land.

'I reckon that was a satisfactory night's work,' Keever called, when they were able to slacken their pace to ease their horses.

'The most satisfactory since the great John Singleton Mosby called on my skills to give the Yankees some worries back in the war,' boasted Ike Jilks. And, for the first time in years, he hooted the blood-curdling notes of the triumphant cry of the Confederate soldiery known as the 'rebel yell'.

'Well, though I wore blue uniform pants in the big war and though Yankee I'll always be, I have to share the feeling with you – you damned rebel!' responded Larry Thorsen, voicing the euphoria felt the by the whole party.

Then they heard a distant crackle of gunfire from the direction of the TT Ranch. It swelled in volume, sending staccato echoes over the rangeland.

Clearly, the little group of defenders at the ranch were experiencing trouble in spades.

CHAPTER SIX

NIGHT ATTACK

Clay Glandon, mounted on a tall horse, was striving to make himself appear impressively general-like in the sober frock-coat he wore to provide a façade of dignity and was flourishing his big Navy Colt. He jogged impatiently around the yard of the Big Three, now filled with restless saddle horses and the whole of his crew, including his two remaining hired triggermen, Froelich and Trotter. They sat in their saddles impassive faced and, as usual, somewhat aloof from the rest of the hands.

Since brute force had so far delivered most of his spoils into Glandon's hands, it formed the major element of his immediate strategy. He sought vengeance against the TT for the killing of

Blackie Harrigan and its defiance of the authority he wielded in Arrow Ridge. He wanted his revenge swiftly and he was out to visit upon the rival ranch nothing more than an overblown version of his attacks on the hapless homesteaders. He planned a crude, swift and destructive swoop on the TT ranch house. It would, Glandon hoped, be such an effective initial blow that the bulk of TT opposition would be quenched early, but his devious mind had hatched a follow-up, a death-blow he believed would be totally devastating.

He was furiously angry at the return of Dan Flagel and his companions with the corpse of Blackie Harrigan. To infuriate him further, not only had Flagel, Sisley and Kerr failed to take any action during the run-in with the TT men in the town, Flagel had sheepishly explained that all Arrow Ridge was talking about the departure of Rufe Wallis and Sam Twigg. The pair had, it seemed, simply up and quit, scooting out of town for unknown regions like a pair of scared jack-rabbits.

Glandon feared the rot was setting in and his grip on this country was slipping, thanks to the defiant action of the TT outfit, and an undermining of his expansive schemes might follow. The hash of Tom Cardigan and his crew needed settling. For Glandon, the only good news out of Arrow Ridge was that Blackie Harrigan had managed to take Will Keever into the realm of death with him. Deprived of its only hired gun, the TT's strength would be significantly reduced although the outfit was well armed thanks to Ike Jilks.

Although Dan Flagel, Sisley and Kerr had been ineffective in the Arrow Ridge affair, Glandon knew their value and that of the rest of the Big Three's hardcases when it came to bullying raids against homesteaders and he wanted a crushing assault of the same pattern against the TT. From his saddle, he fired up his mounted crew, bawling hoarsely, 'Get it through your skulls that this is a war – and I'm leading you into it myself! And we don't have to worry about Keever any more. I'm having no half-measures. I want value for the good money I'm paying you – so let's ride!'

Glandon had carefully ensured that he took no part in the fighting when the fate of the nation was being decided by warring factions: he had concentrated on feathering his nest. Now, however, with his grasping schemes at stake, he was intent on battle. With Glandon, it had to be battle heavily weighted in his favour so, trundling behind the column of riders he led out of the ranch yard, was a wagon with a huge load of hay – a key part of Glandon's plan for a swift reduction of the TT's defences.

With the rangeland fully gathered into the night, they took a circuitous route so as to approach the TT headquarters by a way which would suddenly bring them over the crest of rising land instead of riding conspicuously over a stretch of open terrain.

Glandon and his warlike party were unaware that, at that very time, down by the creek bed elsewhere on Big Three land, four horsemen were heading speedily but cautiously towards the instrument of Glandon's water-rustling, the dam.

The Big Three men pounded through the night bunched together with Glandon in the lead, making a determinedly aggressive show. Close beside him rode Dan Flagel, who had been putting on a blustering front in an attempt to gain some face with Glandon after his failure to make to any stand against Tom Cardigan and his companions in Arrow Ridge.

Slightly behind him jogged the hired gunmen, Froelich and Trotter. Both were stony-faced as usual but certain emotions were surging inside Trotter. Until the day that had just closed, Slim Trotter had a very particular reason for going against the TT. He wanted to be the one who killed Will Keever.

It had to do with the long ago slaying of Cass Chisnall by Keever in the Wyoming range war. Chisnall had once been Trotter's trail partner. In his later years, Chisnall turned bad, nor was Slim Trotter any better, but it had been a different story long before. They were once idealistic young cowpokes, probably as decent as any young men of their day. They turned bad in the harsh times and starvation conditions on the ranges in that brutal winter later remembered as 'the Big Die' when men and cattle perished in never-ending snow and there was wholesale loss of jobs. They stayed bad, hit the owlhoot trail, drifted apart and each went on to establish his own reputation in the thick of spitting guns and powdersmoke.

Much earlier, in their youth on the Dakota ranges, Chisnall staked his own life, yanking Trotter, fallen from his horse, from certain death under a torrent of stampeding beef. Trotter owed every subsequent year of his turbulent existence to Chisnall and never forgot it.'

Through the years, a remnant of honour remained in Slim Trotter and, ever since hearing of Cass Chisnall's end in a gun duel with Will Keever, he had harboured a grudge which he vowed to settle if ever he met up with Keever.

Shortly after Trotter signed up for Glandon's trigger money, Will Keever showed up which seemed almost miraculous to Trotter. He felt that Keever had been delivered into his hands. With the killer of Cass Chisnall on these very Montana ranges, his personal vendetta overrode his gun-wage commitment to Glandon.

He planned to play along with the schemes of the Big Three's owner but his private and strictly unspoken purpose for being on the Big Three's strength now was to get to Will Keever and kill him.

Then came word of Keever's death in a freak duel which had also taken the life of Blackie Harrigan. That Harrigan, whom Trotter and Froelich regarded as a has-been and a windbag, should slay Keever whom Trotter had privately marked out as his own meat, raised bitter chagrin in Trotter. Robbed of what had become his chief reason for a battle with the TT, he rode with the Big Three raiders with the vengeful attitude that action against the rival ranch would at least provide an opportunity to work off his gnawing disappointment.

The party pounded deep into TT territory, swept up a shoulder of land beyond which lay the ranch headquarters at the bottom of the downward slope on the further side of the shoulder. Glandon signalled a halt. The raiders allowed their horses to blow while Glandon took a position before them.

'Form up in line and we'll go over the hill, then down on the house. Start shooting right off. No pow-wowing and no yelling at them to get out. These are not dithering sodbusters, they're cattlemen and they'll fight,' he said in a hoarse whisper.

He began to issue instructions and revealed his ace in the hole.

'We'll have the wagon unhitched, turned the shafts behind, waiting on the hill with six of you handling it,' he directed. 'When the time is ripe, those with the wagon will set the hay afire with lucifers. It's already been treated with plenty of oil. Shove the wagon down the slope, through the yard fence and into the house. If there's any opposition left, it won't last long with the house on fire.'

Up on the log roof of the TT ranch house, Hank Sands, one of Cardigan's doughtiest veterans, was planted as a lookout, sprawled on his stomach. He gripped a Winchester, with a second one from the adequate armoury supplied by Ike Jilks lying beside him. He was the first to spot the arrival of the Big Three raiders.

The ridge facing the house was only just discernible as a black line against the slightly lighter background of the moonless spring sky. Suddenly, Sands heard the thump of approaching horses. He saw a line of silhouettes rise above the horizon and quickly resolve itself into jumbled shapes of big-hatted, wide-chapped horsemen – coming fast.

Sands' first reaction was to gulp in alarm as he realized how many aggressors were advancing on the ranch which, in addition to himself, was defended only by Cardigan, Ted Freed, Shorty Cannon and Chang the cook. Even had Keever, Jilks, Thorsen and Mex Cortez been present, the odds would still look overwhelming. But Hank Sands, who, as a private in the Union Army, had once faced the challenge of Pickett's Virginia division of Confederates charging in a furious wave upon the Union position on Cemetery Ridge at Gettysburg, was not nonplussed for long.

Acting like an old warhorse responding to the scent of battle, he grabbed the spare carbine and, crouching low with a Winchester in each hand, scooted along the roof to where the fieldstone chimney of the house rose out of the gable.

He stood up against the chimney on the offside from the approaching raiders just long enough to bawl down it, '*Here they come, boys! Here they come!*'

The sound of his own voice brought back with a

qualm the memory of his old commander yelling that very same warning across the tensed and wait-ing blue ranks that terrible third and last day at Gettysburg.

He hoped there was not an ominous portent in it as again he shouted down the chimney, '*Here they come, boys! Here they come!*'

The oncoming riders were still a massed and jumbled shadow against the deeper darkness of the night as Hank Sands slithered down against the slant of the ranch-house roof away from the approaching Big Three party. He slowly levelled his Winchester and fired a chance shot at the horsemen.

Even as he was rewarded with a yelp of pain out of their midst, he rolled back until he was closer to the chimney, fired again from this different angle, rolled back again to change his position in case someone among the raiders had pinpointed the spot from which he had just fired.

But the Big Three riders were not up to such strategic thinking at that moment. They were too busy charging down the slope towards the house, which had so far seemed a sitting target.

The initial shot from the roof and the fact that one of their number had been hit was a shock causing some to automatically rein in their

97

animals. The second shot, coming from another angle, gave the impression that there was more than one sniper on the roof and so intensified the degree of confusion.

Old-time military hands among the raiders quickly realized that they might be caught on the downward side of this slope, facing the house and making easy targets. They were without cover with no idea as to the true strength of the opposition yet to open fire in defence of the TT head-quarters.

There was considerable scrambling and confusion among the raiders with some making to haul their animals around and retreat from this exposed position.

Clay Glandon, at their head, now realized the flaw in his generalship: he had taken his force head-on down a slope without knowing the potential of the enemy facing them. With panic flaring in him, it suddenly came to him that Cardigan might have somehow gathered more men than his regular crew. He also began to realize that he had placed his men in an exposed position.

The gravity of his situation was emphasized when the defenders inside the house, crouching behind their barricades of furniture at the windows, reacted to Hank Sands' warning yells and opening shots by firing rapidly at the attackers.

Bullets *whanged* around the Big Three horse-men; an animal screeched and there were ragged yells and curses. Some of the attackers began to fire randomly towards the house while still on the move.

Clay Glandon, waving his Navy Colt ineffectively and yelling panicky orders to draw back, felt the weight of the lesson he had tried to instil into the raiders: that the TT men were not timid, dirt-farm-ing homesteaders, but cowmen, answering the attack in cow-country fashion.

At the house, Hank Sands had changed his posi-tion on the roof again. So far, no Big Three aggres-sor had gathered his wits sufficiently to respond to his sniping and he let fly with another random shot. He grinned as he altered his post yet again.

'Here's another to keep the pot boiling,' he murmured, as he fired once more without taking aim.

Greatly encouraged by the blast of weapons from the men in the house and aware of the confu-sion among the enemy, Hank Sands was almost beginning to enjoy this ruction.

A mere two – Tom Cardigan and Shorty Cannon – were behind the windows, well forted up behind their barricades and firing for all they were worth.

Ted Freed and Chang had established themselves with a good reserve of ammunition at another window from which it would be easy to defend the horses penned nearby in the ranch yard if the attackers attempted to run them off. They were also within good range of the raiders and they added lustily to the fusillade of shots from Cardigan and Cannon.

Outside, the cooler heads among the Big Three raiders were attempting to stand their ground and answer the shots from the house at considerable risk from the defenders' fire.

Glandon's attempt to take the TT ranch house by surprise with an all-out charge had failed. Almost all his men were unhorsed now, scooting back up the slope, trying to save themselves and their animals. All that was in their favour was the cover of night, making any precise aiming of shots by the TT men difficult. Even so, their lead was screeching all around the attacking party and several Big Three men were hit.

Someone gave a chilling, croaking howl, '*Get the hell out of here!*'

This sparked a panic that fed the panic already churning in Clay Glandon. He was out of his saddle, holding his reins with one hand and, with the other, still waving his Colt without having yet

100

fired it. He was all too fully aware that he was dangerously positioned at the front of the mêlée on the slope.

Up on the roof of the house, Hank Sands squinted into the broiling, shadowy action beyond the fenced yard and loosed off a further two shots with a grin of satisfaction, but one of the cooler heads among the attackers had obviously spotted his position and he ducked as a gun barked and a slug screamed close to his head to chip a stone splinter off the chimney stack.

Sands saw that the muzzle-flames from his weapons were probably pinpointing his position. 'Looks like I've done all I can up here,' he mused philosophically. 'There's not enough room to keep ducking around without being hit.'

He slithered down the rear portion of the roof, slung his two carbines across his back and dropped into the ranch yard behind the house.

Just as he hit the ground, he heard a sudden and distinct reverberation blasting out of the night. It came from the Big Three's land. Hank Sands beamed and almost cheered.

'The dam! An explosion from over yonder on the Big Three! Looks like Keever and the others have done it!' he gasped gleefully.

He ran into the house to join the small band of

defenders at the windows, yelling, 'There was an almighty bang over at the Big Three! Sounds like the dam has been blown to hell and gone!'

The defenders gave hoarse cheers while continuing to shoot and Sands joined them, flinging himself behind a breastwork of upturned tables and chairs.

Outside, some Big Three men were returning sporadic fire but the majority were scrambling up the rise with their horses. The attackers, too, had heard the stark blast of the far explosion. Clay Glandon, trying to rally his forces and, at the same time, attempting to place himself out of danger from the firing from the house, turned towards his distant rangeland. He saw a dying crimson and yellow glow in the sky at precisely the spot where he knew the dam and the crude reservoir his men had constructed to hold the stolen water were located. This added a nagging edge to his panic.

He gave a gasping growl of alarm: 'The dam! What the hell has happened at the dam?'

The urge for self-preservation quickly overtook him as a bullet from the ranch house thudded into the earth close to his foot; he let go of the reins of his led horse and went speeding in a half-crouching retreat up the hill.

He found himself in the midst of a jumble of his

men who had likewise hotfooted it up to the crest to escape the blazing windows of the ranch house. Among this disorganised jostle, he discovered his foreman, Dan Flagel, and several others who had swaggered belligerently when they deluded themselves that attacking the TT would be as easy as harassing sodbusters. All were now cowering out of range of the defenders of the ranch house.

Hardly a hero himself, Glandon was aware of the fear that infected them. It was a fear he knew only too well himself as he realized the strategy of his charge on the TT ranch house was a dire failure.

But the fact that this set of bunkhouse toughs, who were taking his gun wages, were proving all but useless in this opening onslaught against the rival ranch, enraged him. In addition, he was fearful that the wholesale confusion would cause desertion in the midst of the action and his anxiety had a curious stiffening effect on his morale, making him attempt a further rallying of his forces. He tried to round them up and reorganize them them to retaliate against the TT crew.

'Yellow!' he yelled. 'Every man jack of you is yellow!'

He charged into the midst of the hands, waving his Navy Colt. 'You spineless bunch!' he roared. 'Don't you run out on me. I'll kill anyone I see running for the tall timber!'

Then he saw his ace in the hole – the heavily laden hay wagon, resting on the crest of the rise, its horse jittering between the shafts, frightened by the shooting from the house.

As more random bullets came blazing out of the ranch house, Glandon put on a spurt, striving to get himself out of range and, while fighting for breath, managing to croak to the men near the crest of the hill. '*The wagon! Get the horse out of the shafts! Set the hay afire! Roll the wagon! Roll it!*'

Dan Flagel and others rushed towards the wagon and began to wrest the horse from between the shafts and there was a flash of light as someone fired a lucifer.

CHAPTER SEVEN

FIRE ON
THE RANGE

Sparked into urgent action by the echoes of distant gunfire from the direction of the TT ranch, Keever and his companions went pounding away from the shattered dam, urging speed out of their already tired horses. They had only a vague idea that the Big Three land was being swamped by water and they did not know what had become of the two defenders, caught by the sudden, over-whelming deluge from the shattered structure.

They rode grim-faced and silent. It was evident that the TT ranch, manned by hardly a handful of defenders, was under attack and sound of distant battle spurred the four to force their lathered horses out of the Big Three territory and across into the TT's range.

They neared the ranch's headquarters and thundered over a hill, the route bringing them on to top of the rise facing the TT ranch house where a dramatic scene was being enacted. On the lip of this hump of land and only yards ahead of them, there was a wagon laden with furiously blazing hay. By its vivid, flaring light, several men were toiling at its trailing shafts, pushing it towards the edge of the crest. As yet, it was lumbering and creaking under their efforts but, once it was fairly on the slope, it would surely roll freely under gravity to trundle down, breach the fencing of the yard and assuredly crash with its fiery cargo into the log house.

The galloping party rode to the edge of the circle of illumination flaring from the blazing hay. The Big Three men at the wagon and their disorganized companions around them, suddenly halted their activities and stared. Three of the four TT men reined, swung themselves out of their saddles gripping their revolvers. Keever snatched his buffalo gun from its scabbard and pitched himself down to the grass. He was dimly aware of faces, painted by the lurid flames from the burning cargo of the wagon. They stared at him aghast and unbelieving. Among them was the florid face of a big man in a black broadcloth suit who could only be Clay Glandon.

Glandon and the rest of the Big Three raiding party had never seen Keever before. He was a legend with a Sharps Special, but he had been slain on the street of Arrow Ridge only hours before. Now they gaped with chilled innards – a ghost had appeared out of the night and the cumbersome weapon identified him. This was the vengeful spectre of Will Keever.

'My God!' called one of them. 'It's Keever! He ain't dead.'

In the midst of the Big Three crew, Slim Trotter heard this exclamation and the hair almost rose on his head.

Trotter had been making himself scarce among the raiders who had sought the safety of the crest and with him was Glandon's other big reputation gunslinger, Karl Froelich. Both men had independently reached the same conclusion: Glandon had bungled his attack from the start. Everything had quickly turned against him and sheer fiasco was unfolding all around the raiders.

Both Trotter and Froelich felt they were rather too good for this blundering brawl. Each considered he embellished his deadly business with some style and the enactment around the TT ranch house was totally without style. It had the effect of making Trotter and Froelich even more aloof from the rest of Glandon's crew.

But Trotter was suddenly alerted by the sound of Keever's name. Powered by his own peculiar sense of honour and his thirst for vengeance, and bearing a naked gun, he moved out of the jostle of men and horses which had moved back from the wagon to avoid the heat of its blazing burden. If Keever was indeed alive and within reach, it seemed that he had been delivered into Slim Trotter's hands after all and Trotter wanted the vengeful pleasure of blasting the life out of him.

He moved as near as was comfortable to the hay wagon and saw Keever through a haze of heat. He was sprawling spread-legged on the ground, aiming his big buffalo gun in the direction of the sluggishly trundling wagon. He was within easy range and Slim Trotter could have killed him there and then at his leisure, but he wanted Keever to know why his life was ending at the point of Trotter's gun. As Trotter's trigger finger pumped bullets into him, he wanted Keever to know it was in payment for the slaying of Cass Chisnall. He wanted Keever to die rueing killing the only worth-while partner Trotter had ever known, in that long ago Wyoming range war.

As things stood, it would be too easy and Keever would never know what hit him or why. So Trotter waited with his gun silent.

Some little distance behind Keever, his companions had also flattened themselves on the ground after leaving their saddles. Almost as soon as the party of dam wreckers hit the earth and just as the astonished men pushing the wagon ceased their exertions, the vehicle began to teeter over the edge of the crest and wobble onto the slope facing the house.

Keever took aim at the slowly turning and creaking wheel closest to him. He loosed a crashing blast and the shell hammered into the heavy wooden rim, tearing away virtually a quarter of the wheel.

The wagon continued to creak onward, shedding flaring clumps of hay. The wheel rolled slowly round until the shattered portion made contact with the earth. Then the wagon halted, shuddered and pitched over to one side. Fiery sections of its cargo began to fall and blow in the slight breeze then the wagon and its flaring burden thudded to the ground.

Yet more blazing hay shot in every direction as

the cargo splashed across the grass in a huge pool of flame that illuminated the scene with dramatic vividness, painting the faces of the dumbstruck men who believed they had just seen the ghost of Keever. All were now stilled in horror, watching the pool of fire spread itself in rapidly travelling streams across the grass now wholly dried out after the recent rains.

They and their frightened horses instinctively surged back from the flames. Trotter among them, lost sight of Keever as a wall of flame and choking smoke flared up between the group of Big Three men and Keever and his companions.

Now, the wooden structure of the wagon was being consumed and it and the hay had become a huge, uncontrollable bonfire, sending out yet more streams of flame across the grassland.

Slim Trotter was somewhere beyond the wall of billowing smoke, lurid flames and shimmering haze of heat which combined to make the landscape a grotesque, hellish picture. He blundered back into the surging company of Big Three men somewhere among whom was Glandon who had initiated this vicious expedition.

And a new fear clutched at the innards of men on both sides of the battle. This had the makings of something none of them ever wanted to experience – *a full-scale, sweeping and all-consuming range-land conflagration!*

It engendered a fear felt by Keever, Thorsen, Elks and Cortez on one side of the wall of fire and the Big Three men on the other side while it set their horses to whinnying and stamping in terror. Keever came up from his lying position feeling fear, anger and not a little guilt. This spreading fire might yet burn the whole of the TT range to a cinder, bringing utter ruin to his brother-in-law and the enterprise he and his wife had striven to create. Keever had caused the wagon to founder and tip over by firing the powerful buffalo shell into its wheel, but it was Glandon and his minions who had brought fire to the range in the first place. Keever felt a savage hatred of the owner of the Big Three who was somewhere beyond the barrier of fire. He wanted to root him out of this country and destroy him as if he were a poisonous growth.

He trudged forward with the buffalo gun slanted across his middle and halted as near to the fire as he dared. Over the crackle of flames and the cacophony of men and horses, he roared in a voice made hoarse by the smoke, '*Glandon – I'm coming for you! Do you hear me? Your dam is blown all to hell and I'm going to finish you, too. I aim to get to the bottom*

111

of your doings in this country. I'll make you spill plenty that'll interest the law including whether you killed your two partners and buried them on your spread! No matter how many gunnies you have around you, I'm going to nail you good!'

On the other side of the barrier of flame, Clay Glandon stood as if paralyzed, watching the flames and still bewildered by the fact that Keever had apparently returned from the dead. His men were surging around him but Karl Froelich was standing near him, immobile as Glandon himself and holding the leathers of his jittery horse. All through the retreat up the rise, he had taken good care to keep a grip on his reins and not to lose his animal.

Froelich was thinking his own cynical thoughts. He had been thinking them for some time and this fiery development was causing certain intentions to solidify in him. He had from the start been mentally apart from Glandon's crude warmaking and he was on the point of turning his back on it and departing in the fashion of Wallis and Twigg. Glandon's bluster about killing any man who ran for tall timber cut no ice with Froelich. He was on the rancher's payroll because of his gun savvy and with that same gun savvy, he could cut Glandon down to size any time he wanted.

Karl Froelich came out of a Pennsylvania

German colony. As a youngster in the Civil War, he had served in a German unit under the command of the Union's expatriate general Franz Sigel. He had ability as a soldier and, with his natural flair for things military, he might have made his mark as a professional army man. But, after the war, his restless spirit took him West.

Froelich turned bad in the rowdy, brawling atmosphere of the cattle-trail towns and emerged as a gunfighter with more brains than the usual run of the breed. Hard times forced him up to the raw Montana ranges to take Clay Glandon's trigger-money but, now, in this fiery chaos, he was considering Glandon's incompetence as a leader of men which he had suspected from the start and which was why he ensured that he was not parted from his horse. The soldier in him knew there were times when retreat had to be considered and, for Karl Froelich, that time was now.

Glandon heard Keever's angry declaration from the other side of the barrier of fire and, with it ringing in his ears, he was trying to make sense of what his men were doing. For they were showing no fight – at least not against the TT outfit. They were fighting the fire. Some had taken off their heavy slickers and were beating the flames with them; others had managed to tear off their leather

113

batwing chaps and they, too, were used as weapons against the fire. Though coughing and spluttering in the acrid smoke, every man was desperately giving his attention to tackling the fire, trying furiously to halt its progress. Every man, that is, except Froelich and Trotter, standing apart, aloof as usual.

Glandon himself had reminded his men that the TT crew were cowmen and not timid sodbusters. As a carpet-bagger, an avaricious Johnny-come-lately outsider who had no ingrained affinity with the wide ranges, he had not grasped that his own crew might be mercenary roughnecks but they, too, were essentially cowmen. Like all of their kind, they had the cattle-wranglers' natural terror of three things: a thundering stampede, either of cattle or buffalo; a flood, which could suddenly rise and swallow man and beast – and the terrifying menace of a rapidly raging fire, tearing its merciless way over a prairie or through a stand of timber. Burned-out ranges meant starvation for cowmen as surely as did the frozen, snowed-up acres of grazeland in those unforgiving weeks of 'the Big Die' which most of them had experienced.

Faced with fire on the rangeland, any cowman would give all his energy to fighting it, which was exactly what the Big Three men were doing now.

Confused, scared and bewildered by the way his plans had so rapidly unravelled, Glandon could not even understand that the concern of his men was that, if not quenched, this fire might even spread so far as the Big Three's own ranges and ruin the graze.

Everything else was forgotten, the fire could not only scorch the land, it could take the lives of all on the scene and Glandon's men were expending all their energy, beating at the flames and even trying to stamp them out with their boots.

And, from the other side of the surging fire, the hoarse bellowing of Keever, the man from the dead, sounded again. '*I'm coming for you, Glandon! I'm going to drive you off these ranges!*'

Glandon had so far been able to hold off total panic but now, with the crew he relied on as his instruments of villainy toiling like demons in the thick of the inferno, giving their whole attention to stopping the spread of the conflagration, his nerve began to give out completely. He felt stripped of his power and abandoned.

From beyond the blazes and smoke, the harsh voice of the gunfighter who had apparently returned to life, came again. '*I'm going to get you, Glandon. I'll bring the law in here – real law, Federal law, not your puppet badge-toters – and you'll answer for your shenanigans!'*

Glandon clutched his Navy Colt ineffectively. He felt Keever, apparently a corpse only hours before, might by some magic suddenly appear on this side of the fiery barrier and he knew he was no match for the man with the buffalo gun and the big-trigger reputation.

The threat of Federal law brought icy panic to his guts. There were affairs the law must not know about. Chiefly, there was the matter of the mysterious deaths of his erstwhile partners, Elias Todd and Charlie Harris, to whom Keever had referred, and the whereabouts of their bodies. Also, there were dealings concerning his plans for expansion after his land-grabbing through tyranny. His schemes for eventual profiteering hand-in-hand with certain lawyers and a certain railroad company were to be found in intimidating papers back at the Big Three headquarters. He must keep them from the eyes of Federal law at all costs.

The remnants of his courage unravelled. Wild-eyed, Clay Glandon looked around for a means of escape and of saving his neck.

CHAPTER EIGHT

PURSUIT

Anger blazed in Keever as fiercely as the fire on the ridge above the TT's headquarters. Clutching his buffalo carbine, he looked around for some means of crossing the barrier separating him from the raiders and their leader.

He was all but consumed by his desire for retribution against Clay Glandon and it took him some time to realize that his companions of the dam raid, Thorsen, Jilks and Cortez, were now beating at the flames with their slickers as were the Big Three crew on the other side of the fiery divide. Furthermore, all shooting had stopped and he turned to see Tom Cardigan, Ted Freed and the rest of the ranch's defenders running up the rise

117

from the house bearing heavy tarpaulin sheets with which to smother the flames. The TT men and those from Glandon's outfit were making common cause against the common enemy, the raging menace of a pastureland fire which might ultimately overwhelm men and cattle.

Still, his desire to pay Glandon for loosing this scourge of the cattlelands to the range where his sister and her husband had laboured to create a flourishing ranch took priority even over the urgency of quenching the flames. He had to get around that sweeping wall of fire and find the owner of the Big Three.

He tried to pierce the smoke and the heat-haze and became dimly aware of groups of loose horses that had shied off to one side, scared by the fire. They were milling about, jittering, snorting and kicking the ground. He hastened towards them. One, a stolid looking mare, allowed him to grab it by the saddle trappings. The animal's rump was branded with the Big Three iron.

'For the first time in my life, I'm turning horse-thief and I'm claiming you,' he told the creature.

On the other side of the partition of fire, Clay Glandon was blundering around. He did not assist his crew who were fully engaged with tackling the outbreak of fire. He saw his foreman, Dan Flagel, with Sisley, Kerr and others who were usually willing to dance attendance on him now oblivious to his presence as they sweated and toiled to beat out the fire. Feeling totally abandoned and thoroughly unnerved, he searched for a mount on which to leave this scene as fast as possible. With nagging anxiety, he wanted to get his hands on the evidence in his safe back at his house and destroy it.

He saw Karl Froelich and Slim Trotter standing off to one side, looking even more aloof than usual. Froelich was holding the reins of his horse, made restless by the conflagration. Glandon rushed towards him.

'Give me that horse, Froelich,' he demanded.

'Go to hell,' responded Froelich. 'I need this cayuse.'

'Meaning you're going to run out?' said Glandon in a quaking croak.

'Sure, just as you are yourself. Only I'm not going because I'm scared like you; I'm going because your game is played out. I'm too damned good for your fool antics and I figure now's the time to quit.'

Fury overrode even the rancher's abject fear and he spluttered, 'I'm paying you good money. You haven't done anything to earn a red cent.'

Froelich curled his lip sardonically. 'You're scared as all hell, ain't you? I heard Keever's hollering. I reckon you really do believe he came back from the dead and I reckon he'll come after you, sure enough. Well, I figure this is the time you need the services of a gunslick worth his salt, so I'll do a deal with you. I'll run with you and give you protection so long as you up the money.'

'Yes, yes,' Glandon breathed. '1 have money back at the house. I want to get back there quick.'

Slim Trotter pricked up his ears. He wanted to get in on this deal. He, too, believed the time had come to run out on his commitment to Glandon, but he wanted to wreak his personal vengeance on Will Keever. His mind began to work overtime. He was sure that Keever would come after the owner of the Big Three. Glandon could be the bait by which he could get Keever out of these chaotic circumstances and into a position where he might be killed on Trotter's terms – the gloating terms under which Keever learned that he was being paid off for killing Cass Chisnall.

Trotter got in on the act. 'I'll help you,' he volunteered. 'There are plenty of Big Three horses running around. I'll catch a couple for us and we'll get the hell out. I'll help you out, Mr Glandon.'

Karl Froelich curled his lip again, sickened by

Trotter's sudden fawning, apparently on the chance of earning more gun money since Froelich knew nothing of Trotter's ulterior motives. He had so far tolerated Trotter's company but he did not like him. There was a streak of inherited Prussian officer-class militarism in Froelich that made him view Trotter as essentially a hayseed cowpoke, a mere peasant.

Still with his superior aloofness, Froelich mounted the horse he had ensured he kept close to him while Glandon stood by. Trotter went off into the swirling smoke and returned leading two horses.

The mare to which Keever had laid claim was kitted out with range-gear: saddle, blanket, rope and a saddle scabbard housing a 1875 model Winchester. Keever left this where it was and mounted the animal. He fumbled in his slicker pocket and found new shells, provided by Ike Jilks. He shoved them into the breech of his weapon which he slanted across the saddle pommel.

The mare shifted uneasily and struck the ground with her hoofs nervously. Keever urged the animal into action. She had the jitters, resulting from the unnerving proximity of fire and obviously knew there was stranger in the saddle. She reacted to his handling by shaking her head and snorting in annoyance.

Impatient to pursue Glandon though he was, Keever knew it would take a little time for horse and rider to understand each other. Gradually, he coaxed the animal out of her nervous shifting around and swung about to ride the length of the streams of flames separating him from the crew of Big Three men and their leader.

Using his spurs judiciously, he set the mare to trotting forward briskly. He left the TT toilers against the fire behind and eventually rounded the fiery barrier to come upon a similar scene where the Big Three crew were battling the flames. They were blackened by smoke and were batting at the fire with slickers and chaps and even their hats. By now, most of them had scorched shirts and some were close to near exhaustion but they were having some success in stopping the spread of the fire.

Keever looked around as best he could in the swirling smoke but saw no sign of Clay Glandon. He made out the solid form of Dan Flagel whom he remembered only too well from the run-in at Arrow Ridge. Flagel was stamping out flames with scorched and blackened boots.

'Where's Glandon?' shouted Keever.

Flagel looked at him with eyes red-rimmed and

streaming. 'Damned if I know and damned if I care!' he retorted harshly. He waved a hand vaguely. 'He rode off yonder with Froelich and Trotter. They can go to hell for all I care. I want to lick this fire.'

For a brief instant, Keever almost admired Dan Flagel. He had fully earned his reputation as a swaggering bully who, claiming to defend the cattlemen's right to the ranges, intimidated and ran off harmless homesteaders. He was powered by a Montana cowman's fanatical belief that this lush country was created for his kind alone and now, the better part of the essential cattleman in him was causing him to make a stand against the curse of rangeland fire. He and other Big Three men were allied with the TT crew against a deadly common enemy.

Flagel paused in his efforts briefly and, through coughs and splutterings, said, 'I'm damned if I know how you came to life again, Keever, but Glandon ran out on us right after he told us we were all yellow! If you're a ghost, I hope you haunt him all the way to hell!' He returned to his strenuous fire-fighting.

Keever wished he was mounted on his familiar but now exhausted roan as the mare danced fractiously when he swung her about, trying to guess which way Glandon, Froelich and Trotter had fled. A skittish, nervy mount was hardly an advantage, but he hoped the animal would soon become accustomed to a new man in the saddle.

Glandon must surely be headed for the Big Three headquarters with the two gunmen who were plainly the last of his allies. Keever was unfamiliar with the open and trail-less range but he set off in what he hoped with the general direction.

Fingers of dawn were beginning to streak the sky as he left the scene of the fire and he began to realize how weary he had become. He had been in all-out, energy-sapping action for hours. His bones were aching and he knew he would soon be craving sleep.

He tried to steel himself and keep alert with his burning desire to make good his threat to bring Glandon before genuine United States law for his many depredations, but, in particular, his ace-in-the-hole trick which had brought fire to the TT ranges.

In his short time at the TT, Keever had formed a powerful affinity with the outfit and he was aware that he had a strong emotional stake in it. His sister slept in its soil close to the house she and her husband had built on the ranges they had worked into a flourishing enterprise.

Keever, who was really Jack Travers, was bitterly conscious of having failed Thalia in the past as he had failed his whole family and he had come to Montana in a spirit of reparation because he heard there was a wrong to be righted where the TT was concerned. Thalia would doubtless not have admired his past lifestyle or his skills in man-tracking and man-killing, but he owed it to her and to Tom Cardigan to use those skills in saving their ranch and he now had a near obsessive desire to bring Glandon to justice.

He pushed onward under the new dawn, controlling the mare in her occasional bouts of temperament by yanking on the reins or kneeing her ribs. All the time, his vision alternated between the flat horizon ahead and the ground where he might find some sign of recent passage by horses. Glandon, Froelich and Trotter could not have had a great start on him but he had no idea as to the exact route they had taken.

He pondered the question of Froelich and Trotter standing by Glandon. Probably, Glandon was aware of his own inadequacy as a fighter. His lawless achievements resulted from his employment of others' gun skills and brawn and, when it came to protecting himself, he needed the same kind of hired might. Froelich and Trotter's motives for sticking to him now could only be mercenary.

They were gunsharps with reputations and the real skill of each was an unknown quantity to Keever. Possibly each would prove an even more dangerous proposition than Blackie Harrigan who, at the last, showed he had speed.

'But I'll settle their hash,' Keever promised the mare, patting the side of her neck. 'Provided I don't fall asleep before I get to them!'

He was increasingly conscious that the fatigue seeping into his bones could blunt his reactions if it came to battling it out with the three, particularly the skilled Froelich and Trotter. His quarry must also be weary, but they had a three to one advantage over him and they were more familiar with the landscape. With every hoof-fall of his nervous steed, it was drummed into his consciousness that he was up against three men yet to be located in a vast expanse of territory.

The sun came up with the suddenness usual in the plains country. It spilled bright, broad light over the land and the gathering warmth strengthened Keever's stamina and sharpened his sensitivities. He rode down a slope, taking care not to push his tetchy mount too hard.

Then his spirits rose as he saw trampled grass ahead. Horses had passed over it only recently, marking the direction towards a further ridge. Keever squinted towards it but saw no sign of riders. They must have been travelling fairly fast, but could not be too far over that ridge, he reasoned.

He pressed the mare onward and was soon rewarded by the discovery of fresh horse droppings.

'I'm close,' he muttered, kneeing the animal's ribs. 'Move quick – and don't get ornery on me!'

The animal behaved herself, responding easily to his urgings as he attempted to make more haste. He reached the lower slope, pushed up it, gained the crest and spotted the three jogging horsemen some distance down the far side. As yet, they were unaware that he was on their backtrail. He hurried the mare down the far side of the ridge to prevent the animal and himself from being skylined on the high crest.

Fatigue was taking the edge off his usually alert sensibilities but he was driven on by his savage desire to avenge the attack on the TT. It hardly registered with him that he was heading into a situation where he was outnumbered three to one; he intended to plunge ahead in pursuit of Glandon and his henchmen with all the power he could force out of his unreliable and skittish mount.

Just as Keever reached the flatter land at the base of the ridge, Slim Trotter turned in his saddle and saw him.

'Keever's right behind and gaining on us with that damned buffalo gun!' he yelled.

He raked his mount with his spurs and his companions followed suit.

Clay Glandon turned, wild-eyed, to see the pursuer now urging his mare to further effort. He was haunted by the eerie notion of this man, returned from the dead, being now hot on his heels. He had agonized thoughts of retribution coming from beyond the veil of death. There were other dead men on his conscience: his partners Elias Todd and Charlie Harris. Glandon had arranged their deaths and knew where their bodies were buried.

Glandon crouched forward over his saddle horn, keeping as flat as possible in case Keever let fly with his high calibre weapon. His two hired gunmen, galloping one on either side of him, seemed as fearful of shells from the buffalo gun as he was himself. Glandon was too scared and too preoccupied with headlong flight to even draw the Navy Colt of which he made such a show at the raid on the TT. He panted almost whimperingly, 'Why don't you two fire on him?'

128

'He's out of range,' replied Slim Trotter. 'We couldn't hit him with handguns from this distance.' Then, even as he said it, a logical fact dawned on him. 'But he can't handle that carbine travelling at that speed. It's too heavy to level from a fast horse,' he added.

'And he won't backshoot us, anyway,' put in Karl Froelich, on what sounded suspiciously like a note of admiration for their pursuer.

Trotter turned to look back and saw that, while Keever had gained on them, he was still out of comfortable range.

Even as Trotter's head was still swivelled around, Keever's fractious mare was spooked into playing him false. A small possum came leaping out of the grass and across the path of the fast travelling and already highly keyed-up horse. The mare jerked to a abrupt halt and, shuddering all over, it reared, sending Keever out of the saddle. He pitched to the ground like a sack of wet sand.

Landing on his right side, he lay there, winded, dazed and with his right arm pinned under him. The buffalo gun was sent spinning from across the saddle pommel to fall on the other side of the mare.

Trotter witnessed the mishap with glee rising in him. Keever was lying on the ground and, in that

129

position, unable to draw his Colt, holstered and pinned down by the weight of his body, while the buffalo gun was some distance from him.

Slim Trotter saw his chance. His hope for this pursuit to turn into mere bait to lure Keever into a position where he could be killed with ease had materialized.

Keever was at last delivered into his hands.

Trotter's lips were drawn back in a leer as he reined his lathered mount and turned it about, drawing his sixgun as he did so.

'I'm going back. He's on the ground and I aim to kill him,' he snarled triumphantly. Glandon, driven by anxiety, paid him no heed and continued strenuously urging his horse onward but Froelich, frowning, watched Trotter put on a spurt towards the fallen man.

Trotter reached Keever, drew rein and swung out of his saddle. Flourishing his gun and grinning, he walked towards Keever. Still winded and still with his right arm pinned beneath him, Keever was aware of the gunman looming into his vision with his face contorted into a leer. He was also dimly conscious that, in the background, Froelich had turned his mount, trotted briskly towards them, halted the animal and dismounted.

He struggled to free his right arm from the

under the weight of his body while Trotter stood over him, levelling his gun at his head.

'I'm paying you out, Keever,' he pronounced slowly with his eyes glittering. 'This is your come-uppance for killing Cass Chisnall, the only worth-while partner I ever had. He yanked me out from under a stampede years ago and I figure I owe him a big debt. Yeah, I suppose it's a debt of honour. Honour! That sounds mighty good, and killing you will feel mighty good. I'm going to enjoy it!'

He cocked the gun with its mouth trained on Keever's head.

Slim Trotter was going to take his time about this slaying.

CHAPTER NINE

DEATH ON
THE TRAIL

Keever squirmed and managed to get his arm free from under his body but, with his right side still pressed against the earth, his holstered gun was inaccessible.

There was a sudden movement to his right. Keever saw Karl Froelich, now afoot, come into view beside Trotter. Abruptly, Froelich made a lightning move for his holstered pistol.

'*Keever!*' he called. '*Catch!*'

Something metallic streaked through the air in Keever's direction and Trotter's attention was distracted for an instant. Making an instinctive gunfighter's move with his newly freed hand, Keever grabbed the object.

It was Froelich's sixgun.

Even as Trotter swung his attention back to the sprawling Keever and a split second before he had a chance to trigger his gun, Keever fired upward.

Slim Trotter stiffened, dropped his gun, crumpled at the knees and collapsed to the ground with a look of utter surprise printed on his face.

Still half stunned and with his whole being aching with fatigue, Keever began to scramble upwards. He saw Froelich standing before him, nodding approvingly.

'Honour,' he commented drily. 'Trotter preached of honour just as he was about to shoot a man who was down and helpless. There's no honour in that. And there was a time when I thought that man had some style. Sometimes I'm ashamed of the company I've kept. I have plenty of crimes to my name but the plain murder of some-one helpless on the ground isn't among them. I hope I still have the tattered remains of a soldier's honour. Ask where you will and any honest man will tell you Karl Froelich was straight and fair in his gunplay.'

Keever walked towards Froelich, proffering his gun and striving to recover from his surprise. 'I'm obliged to you,' he gasped.

Froelich took the weapon and holstered it. 'You talked of bringing United States' law here, Keever,' he said. 'The law has nothing on me for anything I did here. Glandon accused me of doing nothing and that's the truth. I took his money but, most of the time, I stood around feeling disgusted with myself for being in his employ. Oh, I was ready to take more of his money right up to a few minutes ago, but Trotter told me he aimed to kill you after you were thrown. He turned back with the intention of doing it and I changed my mind about being involved with him and Glandon. If you want to know what Glandon is up to, he's aiming to get at papers at the Big Three. I figure he knows the jig is up and wants to destroy them.'

He laughed in his sardonic fashion. 'I aim to ride for the far country unless you feel I should be stopped. Then it'll be you and me drawing on each other fair and square. I reckon we're both pretty well dog tired but if you figure you have something to settle, I'm ready. It'll be fair and square, though. I'll let you catch your breath.'

Froelich took a gunfighter's spread-legged stance with his right hand hanging loose just above his holster.

Keever, panting, stared at him and, after a second

of tense silence, said, 'I'm not likely to want to smoke it out with a man who saved my life.'

'Now that,' stated Froelich gravely, 'is real honour. I reckon you and me are of the same kind. Maybe we can claim some real style but I figure our day is coming to an end.' He touched the brim of his hat, returned to his horse, mounted and rode off, angling away eastward while Clay Glandon, galloping alone, had continued ahead in the direction of his ranch.

Keever watched Froelich go, knowing that, for the first time in his career, he had refused to answer a gunfighter's challenge.

Walking away from Trotter's huddled body, he found the mare still quivering nervously. He calmed the animal, collected his Sharps carbine from where it had fallen and remounted. Karl Froelich was becoming a dwindling lone horseman, riding off to what ever destiny awaited him. Clay Glandon had disappeared over a ridge in the distance but Keever knew the general direction of his flight and he resumed the pursuit, at first pacing the mare easily, giving her time to recover from her fright.

Glandon semed to be making good speed though Keever knew both he and his horse must be tiring rapidly.

Up ahead of him, Glandon was all too aware of his abandonment. Trotter and Froelich had gone and, in his panicky haste, he had not even looked back to see what had become of them. He had heard a single shot echoing back and he hoped it marked the end of Keever, a victim of Trotter's murderous intention. But Glandon was taking no chances on turning back to find out. Consumed by his desire to get out of this country as rapidly as he could, headlong flight was all he thought about.

He had badly overplayed his hand with the raid on the TT and the flimsy apparatus of law represented by Wallis and Twigg whom he controlled, no longer existed. Now, Keever, backed by Tom Cardigan, would surely make good on his threat to hit him with the powerful force of Federal law.

Canada! He thought in sudden desperation. *If I can make it over the border into Canada, I'll be clear of US law.*

There was plenty of precedent for men from these northern ranges with prices on their heads evading the clutches of United States' law by high-tailing for Canada. But, first, he must get at the incriminating documents in his safe. If they became evidence in the hands of US lawmen, he might still be pursued through the US authorities acting through an alliance with Canada's doggedly relentless North-West Mounted Police.

Running for Canada made eminent sense to his labouring wits. There were horses in the corral at the ranch – spirited cow ponies. If he reached the Big Three, he could remount on a fresh animal and strike out for the border with the advantage of a fresh horse where Keever's mount must surely be as severely fatigued as the one on which he himself was now saddled.

He saw a stand of cottonwoods ahead of him, and knew he was nearing a point on his land which led to a speedy route to the ranch house. He forced his panting horse towards the trees.

He traversed the stand of timber and rode down the slope on the further side. This route brought him to the dim but distinguishable backtrail that offered a short cut to the house.

He chanced an anxious backward glance. There was no sign of Keever.

The pursuer was, in fact, some considerable distance behind the stand of timber, slowed by the behaviour of the nervy mare which had taken to periodically dancing to one side as if scared of some other creature jumping across her path.

'The only time I ever stole a cayuse with some-body else's brand on its rump, I had to pick you,' growled the frustrated Keever, trying to rein the animal into calmer behaviour.

He saw the clump of cottonwoods on its rise of land, forced his reluctant steed up to them, thinking the grove would offer a viewpoint from which he might spot Glandon.

From among the trees, he looked down and saw not Glandon, but a narrow trail, snaking off around a shoulder of land.

It bore hoof tracks which looked fresh. Glandon must have taken that trail and ridden out of sight around the shoulder. Keever grunted with satisfaction. Such a trail could be a route to the Big Three. He spurred the mare on.

Well ahead of him, Clay Glandon was nearing his ranch headquarters. He had taken the whole complement of his bunkhouse to attack the TT, leaving only two behind. They were the outfit's scrawny cook, Greasy Snead, and the blacksmith, Al Slatters, who knew horses even if he was somewhat dim in the wits.

Encouraged by having lost sight of Keever and bolstered by the hope that, whatever had since happened to the now missing Trotter and Froelich, Keever might have been killed when they dallied with him on the trail, Glandon pushed his tiring horse to further effort along the trail. He saw

138

the stone chimney of the ranch house rise over the horizon.

Standing in the ranch yard, Al Slatters saw him approach. He stared open-mouthed at the spectacle of the rancher, returning alone, red-faced, sweating and on a weary, lathered mount after leaving at the head of the raiding party with such belligerent swaggering. His once neat broadcloth suiting was scorched and crumpled and he looked flustered and badly rattled.

The short and squat form of Greasy Snead, the cook, issued from the cookhouse door.

'Mr Glandon – what's been happening? Where's everybody else? We heard a hell of a racket off yonder on the range in the night and we saw smoke—' he began.

'Shut up!' snapped Glandon, almost jumping out of his saddle. 'Slatters, get this saddle switched to a cow pony, pronto. I want the best one in the corral – the fastest – and I want him damned quick!'

'Sure, Mr Glandon,' responded Al Slatters in his dull way.

'Well, do it! Move, damn you!' roared Glandon.

He almost ran to the door of the house, fumbling in a pocket as he went. Al Slatters scooted off to the big corral at one side of the

139

house where the ranch's remuda of working horse-flesh was penned.

Glandon hastened through the well-appointed rooms to the back chamber he used as an office, holding a key. He dropped to his knees before the safe in a corner and opened it. He began to sort through papers and folders frantically. He glanced quickly at several and began to fold them and stuff them inside his tightly buttoned waistcoat then stood and hastened back to the yard.

A bewildered and scared-looking Al Slatters was holding a stocky little calico pony he had worked fast to saddle.

'He's a mighty good one, Mr Glandon. Got plenty of energy,' ventured Slatters.

Glandon, still securing the papers inside his vest with one hand, made no answer but hauled himself into the saddle, turned the pony's head and spurred the animal forward.

'Mr Glandon, where are you going?' asked the usually subservient Greasy Snead now emboldened by the unusual circumstances.

'A long ways north,' snorted Glandon, as he sent the pony pounding out of the yard.

Al Slatters considered the rancher's departing back with an even greater degree of his habitual puzzlement. 'Maybe he means Canada,' he said.

'D'you figure he means Canada, Greasy?'

'If he does, he's in a hell of a hurry to get there,' shrugged Snead. 'If he'd waited awhile, I could have fixed him some grub for the journey.'

Snead and Slatters were still standing in the ranch yard in bewilderment, trying to fathom Glandon's behaviour and the disappearance of the raiding party he led out the previous night, when there came the sound of another approaching rider. A gaunt figure on a lathered and heaving mare which Al Snead at once recognized as one of the Big Three's own animals came through the gate. He had a buffalo carbine slanted over his saddle pommel which caused instant alarm in two men.

'Hey, you're Keever, ain't you?' squawked Snead. 'I thought you were—'

'—Dead,' finished Keever harshly. 'Well, I'm not. Where's Glandon?'

'Gone,' supplied Al Slatters in a quivering voice as he recalled rumours both of Keever's fast trigger reputation and the local fame already earned by his buffalo carbine. 'He's gone, shoving papers inside his vest, fast as all get out on a fresh pony from the remuda. Said he was going a long ways north.'

'We figure he meant Canada, Mr Keever,' said Greasy Snead.

'Canada? That means he went due north, does-n't it? So far as I know anything about this country, once he crosses the Milk River he'd soon be in Canada,' said Keever, swinging the barrel of his carbine towards the pair meaningfully.

'Sure. He'd head off along the creek for a spell, ford it and keep going north,' said Snead, eager to help at the sight of the buffalo gun.

'Do you have another fresh pony in your remuda? Get me one, pronto. This mare's nearly all in,' barked Keever, climbing down from the saddle.

'Sure thing, Mr Keever,' quaked Slatters, scoot-ing for the corral again.

Though not well endowed with intellect, Al Slatters was a good blacksmith and a competent horse-wrangler. He was proud of the quality of horses he kept at the Big Three and the cow pony on which Will Keever sped out of the ranch yard was a vigorous little animal. Though Keever was himself wearied by his long exertions, he felt a renewal of energy in having the creature under him.

He pressed northward, remembering Froelich's information concerning Glandon's intention to snatch incriminating papers from his headquar-ters. Plainly, those were the documents with which he left the ranch. It was essential to catch him on this side of the Canadian line with the evidence on him.

Keever followed the route vaguely indicated by Snead and, at length, saw the glitter of the waters of the creek in the distance. Snead had said Glandon would follow it and then ford it. Encouraged, he kneed more effort out of the pony.

Ahead of him, Clay Glandon was sending his cow pony streaking over a rise on the other side of which was the route along the creek that would bring him to the shallow point where he could ford the water.

He went pounding down the further slope, then yanked his rein hard, making the animal slither forward to a halt. Full in the path of horse and rider there was something that had never been there before – a vast expanse of water, swamping a great tract of land and totally blocking his escape.

Glandon remembered confusedly that, in the midst of his attack on the TT, he heard an explosion coming from the direction of his own land. Something had happened to release a heavy volume of pent-up water from the dam further along the creek, causing the watercourse to overflow to a phenomenal degree. In fact, as well as sending water flowing within its natural bed and through the TT land once more, the explosion had sent a residue into this portion of the Big Three range and a configuration of the land made it lodge at this crucial point in Glandon's path.

Glandon did not know the depth of the water and, snarling obscenities, he glowered at it from his saddle.

Then he heard the distant thump of a horse, growing louder. Keever was catching up with him. Panic drove him to force the pony forward into the water, hoping he might be able to ford the vast pool.

The water proved deeper than Glandon at first thought and it was soon almost up to the pony's belly.

Snorting a protest, the animal shook its head violently. Then, sensing that it was in danger of drowning, it balked, rearing back, frightened to go further. Glandon, hearing the pounding of the approaching horseman growing yet louder, felt his feet slithering from his stirrups and he was abruptly unhorsed. He went splashing into the water with his arms flailing.

As the pony instinctively turned about and began a laboured return to dry land, Glandon went under the surface, came up and floundered backward, placing himself in an even greater depth. Then a chilling truth came to his fraught consciousness – *he could not swim!*

With the blind panic of a non-swimmer out of his depth, he began to whirl his arms ineffectively, spluttering and gurgling with the breath gusting out of him. He went down but fought his way up to the surface again.

Then into his blurred, watery view came a vision of Will Keever like something out of a grotesque nightmare.

Keever was kneeling on a spit of dry land close to where Glandon and the pony had plunged into the water. He was levelling his buffalo gun directly at him.

Glandon's wild panic subsided for an icy instant as it came to him that he was drowning in water he had attempted to rustle from the TT – at the same time, the man from the south-west was about to kill him from close quarters with his high calibre weapon.

CHAPTER TEN

RETRIBUTION

'Grab the gun!' yelled Keever. 'Grab hold of the barrel!'

Scared and almost disoriented though he was, Clay Glandon realized that Keever, holding the carbine with both hands, was extending it at arm's length as a lifeline. He made a desperate, splashing and wallowing progress towards Keever's position, flung out both arms and took hold of the barrel of the weapon with such force that he almost pulled Keever into the water.

Keever hauled back with all his might, dragging the rancher's considerable bulk towards him. Glandon slithered on to the solid earth. Gasping, wheezing and rendered almost lifeless by his exer-

146

tions in the water, he lay face down looking like a beached whale in his incongruous suit of black broadcloth.

Keever recovered his own breath, knelt beside Glandon and turned the rancher over on his back.

'You have papers inside your vest,' he declared. 'I want them. They'll be wet but still readable, I hope.'

Showing no concern for the gasping, near exhausted Glandon, he unbuttoned his vest and pulled out the wad of papers, then pushed them into the ample pocket inside his slicker.

He rose, stood over Glandon with the carbine levelled at him.

'Get up, and this time, I don't aim to use this gun to save you. Try any smart moves with me and I'll kill you with it!'

Under the threat of the carbine, he made Glandon rise and, after snatching the Navy Colt from his belt and flinging it disdainfully into the water, forced him to make his gasping, stumbling and dripping way to his cow pony.

Glandon had just about enough energy to mount the animal and Keever climbed into the saddle of his own mount. He made the defeated rancher spur his animal forward and rode behind him with his carbine trained on his back.

'Head for your place – and keep looking to your front,' ordered Keever.

Back at the Big Three yard, Snead and Slatters were still standing around in a bewildered state since it seemed that everyone else connected with the outfit had now disappeared from the face of the earth. They saw the approach of the two riders, one of them the bedraggled and soaking wet rancher who plainly ruled the roost in this vicinity no more.

On his first arrival at the ranch, Keever had taken the measure of the cook and the blacksmith and considered they were hardly the type to give him any trouble. From his saddle behind the rancher's pony, he shouted, 'Hey, you two. There's a buckboard yonder. Get a horse into the shafts. You're coming with your boss and me.'

'Where are we going?' asked Greasy Snead querulously.

Keever, feeling close to utter exhaustion but triumphant, had to stifle a yawn, as he answered, 'To the TT, so jump to it.'

At the TT ranch, the grassland was no longer afire and what had been the blazing hay wagon was now a charred and smouldering wreck. In a blackened and smoking landscape, men from the opposing

148

sides were near exhausted and heaving for breath. The raiders might be bunkhouse toughs and not likely to receive much friendship from the TT hands but, jointly, the forces from both ranches had tackled and beaten the flames with frantic fanaticism.

With Clay Glandon off the scene, the raiders lost all incentive to fight. They now had nothing to gain and had capitulated wearily.

Dan Flagel was now being regarded as leader of the raiding party and was not flattered by that distinction. He and others were lying on a patch of burned-out ground recovering their breath and Tom Cardigan, Ted Freed, Chang, Jilks, Cortez and others, all fighting their own exhaustion, were standing over them with drawn firearms.

There was the sobering fact of three of the raiders lying dead on the slope before the TT ranch house while three or four others had flesh wounds of varying degrees. By contrast, the defence of the TT ranch was so well managed that the outfit had suffered no casualties.

'Hell, Mr Cardigan,' said Flagel in an almost wheedling voice. 'These boys ain't about to give any trouble. It was Glandon who got us into this mess and then ran out on us. There's no profit in any of this any more – there's nobody to pay us.'

149

'And I suppose you'll make out you're all innocent as babies, even though you set out to burn down my house and ruin me,' growled Cardigan.

'And you could have burned down my cookhouse and destroyed my full sets of Emerson and Shakespeare,' hooted Chang the literary cook, standing guard in the background.

'But we helped save your range,' wheedled Flagel. 'We did our best to save it. We're cattlemen after all.'

Inwardly, Tom Cardigan had to concede that point. Most of these men had no long-term history with the Big Three. They were mostly unsavoury drifters, recently hired. But, in their bones, they were still cow-wranglers who knew that healthy ranges signified a living for cow-wranglers. Cardigan was determined, however, that they should face justice.

Suddenly, from the trail leading to the ranch yard, there came a hubbub of voices and the sound of horses and wheels.

A motley company was approaching, some on horseback, some riding mules and others in buckboards. They were mostly male but there were some women among them. All carried some kind of weapon. Pistols, shotguns and even archaic squirrel guns were in evidence.

They advanced in a purposeful stream and Cardigan realized they were the folk of Arrow Ridge. It seemed the whole town had turned out in a body.

'What's this procession about? It looks like most everyone in Arrow Ridge is here,' he called, as the party came within earshot.

'They are – all except those who were in Glandon's pocket and they're making themselves powerful scarce,' grinned one man in a buckboard whom Cardigan believed to be a sodbuster dispossessed by Glandon. The man added, 'Some of us homesteaders who'd been hoorawed off our holdings by the Big Three were camped down by Thorny Creek, biding our time, hoping for a chance to hit Glandon in some way. Damned if Rufe Wallis and his blamed fool deputy didn't come passing through, riding like all get-out. They had no badges and were scuttling away like a pair of bats out of hell.

'We got no sense out of 'em. They just kept moving and it was plain something was wrong. Some of our boys went into town and it looked like Glandon's hold on this country was going to hell in a handbasket.'

'Sure,' put in another citizen. 'His lawmen deserted him; Ike Jilks had defied him and taken

151

off with his whole stock, seemingly to the TT, and that Will Keever fellow dropped that gunfighter Harrigan out on the street. Too bad Keever was killed. There was a rumour that Dan Flagel was heard threatening that Glandon would settle with the TT right after Harrigan was shot. In the night, we all heard shooting and an explosion away over on the range and saw signs of fire out this way. We figured the TT was being attacked. It seemed time us Arrow Ridge folk took a hand in things, so everyone ready for a fight was rounded up.'

Another newcomer piped up apologetically, 'That took some time, so we've showed up kind of late, but we figured we should reclaim our town and this country from Glandon. We might look a Johnny-come-lately bunch but we're willing to fight to give this whole place a new start. To our shame, we didn't stand up to Glandon before now but it sure looks like you have this Big Three bunch hogtied. I reckon we have enough guns to help you hold 'em down.'

'Yeah,' rumbled another. 'We should have done some fighting before now.'

'You still have fighting to do for your own good,' came a voice from the trail behind the new arrivals.

The whole company turned and saw a buckboard approaching. It was driven by Al Slatters, Clay Glandon's blacksmith, with Greasy Snead, seated beside him.

Astonishingly, huddled in the well of the wagon was the wet and badly scared owner of the Big Three, accompanied by Will Keever, believed by all Arrow Ridge to be dead. Keever looked weary but alert and was holding his famed buffalo gun trained on Clay Glandon.

Keever considered the company from Arrow Ridge, all now looking aghast at what they thought was the wraith of a dead man, holding the detested Glandon captive. Among them he saw the owner of the restaurant on a wagon with the wife who prepared such good food beside him, and the old-timer whom he had met on first arriving in town was there, humping a Spencer rifle.

'Mr Keever,' called the homesteader in the buckboard. 'You remember me, Jim Steeples. You met me and the wife and kids when you arrived. Glandon's bunch had just run us off our place.'

Keever nodded, remembering the cold dawn when he approached the town and encountered the fleeing dispossessed family.

'I remember you,' he called. 'I reckon you can start putting your roots down on your homesteads again. Everyone has a chance of making these parts worth living in. You can do it best by forming a citizens' committee. You can take Glandon, but don't get ideas about lynching him. Stick him in the Arrow Ridge gaol for now. I'd say there are enough of you to hold the rest of his crew, too. There are US Marshals in Helena who need contacting to bring some real law here. And, eventually, you'll need a properly elected council and a town marshal and deputies worth the name.'

Tom Cardigan, as surprised as the Arrow Ridge folk by this turn of events, pushed his way to Keever's buckboard and called, 'Darn it, Will, I was worried about you after you disappeared on Glandon's tail. I never figured you'd haul him in this way.'

'I owe it to you, Tom,' grinned Keever. 'I feel pretty bad about shooting out that wagon wheel. That's what caused the grass fire.'

'Sure, but it saved the house from burning,' said Cardigan. 'That buffalo gun turned out to be pretty useful.'

'I figure we can safely leave this bunch to these Arrow Ridge folk,' stated Keever and, indeed, a party of the townsmen, glorying in their new found unity and civic pride, were already disarming the defeated men while others took charge of the bedraggled Glandon.

Coming down from the wagon, Keever produced the wad of documents. 'These'll help some when the wheels of justice start to move,' he told Cardigan. 'Glandon was trying to escape into Canada with them so they must be plenty incriminating. Maybe we'll also find out the truth about what happened to the two who were in partnership with him.' He yawned and added, 'And now, I aim to get some sleep!'

Keever and Tom Cardigan stood at Thalia's neat grave in the land she had come to love, each thinking his own thoughts for a few silent moments. It was the day after the débâcle at the TT, fresh, with golden sunshine and a pleasant breeze. Cardigan remembered how the breathtaking beauty of this land captured his young bride on the spring day he first brought her to it. Its promise had been marred by violent and bloodthirsty greed. Cardigan felt the very soil in which Thalia lay had been violated but a menacing veil had now been lifted from it.

Clay Glandon and his fellow captives were at Arrow Ridge, held securely by the newly formed and doggedly determined temporary citizens' committee; old Doc Walker, the nearest medical man, had been brought from neighbouring

Cragsburg to attend to the wounded and the three corpses were lodged in the livery stable awaiting the attention of the coroner. Arrow Ridge had no telegraph but the US Marshal's office in Helena had been contacted through the Cragsburg telegraph. Proud new Arrow Ridge was bringing order to this isolated and previously blighted location.

Cardigan and Keever eventually turned and walked down the hill towards the house. 'Thalia would have enjoyed a morning like this, Will,' breathed Cardigan. 'It's a great day for doing meaningful things.'

'It's Jack, now, Tom, Jack Travers,' said his brother-in-law. 'Thalia wouldn't have wanted to own anyone of Will Keever's kind, with his gunfighter's reputation. Keever is over and done with – he's just as dead as if Blackie Harrigan really did finish him off in Arrow Creek.'

Tom Cardigan nodded. 'Sure, but I think you underestimate Thalia's sympathies. She had a big heart and was big on understanding. I figure she'd have welcomed you home, even as Will Keever. And you *have* come home and I hope you'll stay because I have a proposition. Seems to me you more than earned a big stake in the TT and I want you in as a business partner. What do you say?'

Jack Travers looked bewildered for a moment

then gasped. 'I never saw myself as a rancher but it's an overwhelming offer and I'm in with you without hesitation.'

Tom Cardigan thrust out his hand and they shook. 'Good,' he grinned. 'What we have to do around here in future will occupy us some. Things are going to change in this country. If the railroad ever does come through, it'll do so on decent, legitimate terms not on a history of intimidation, stolen land and rustled water. It'll be a boon to cattlemen and homesteaders alike. Meantime, we have to think about putting the TT into shape again. Maybe we'll have to hire a few new hands because, before we know it, we'll have to cope with a round-up.'

Travers said: 'Talking of doing meaningful things, pretty soon, I'll take a walk to the creek. I have a chore to perform.'

'A chore?' asked Cardigan.

'Sure. I'm going to get rid of this buffalo gun and forget about it.'

Cardigan gasped. 'Get rid of your buffalo gun? Hell, it's part of your personality. It's made you famous around these parts.'

Jack Travers grinned. 'It's served its purpose. Not long ago, Ike Jilks said those weapons were getting kind of obsolete. He was right. The buffalo have mostly been wiped out and some say that was a crime. The Indians certainly do, the buffalo being their chief source of everything they needed to survive. Buffalo guns are going out with the buffalo and those who hunted them into extinction. Mine was given to me in Apache Wells by an ex-buffalo hunter, an oldster who knew the day of his kind was over. I locked him in a cell because he got falling-down drunk.'

'And he still made you a gift of the gun?' asked Tom Cardigan.

'Sure, he was grateful because I treated him right and, when he'd sobered up, we yarned some and I learned he was a plenty wise old bird.

' "Take this here Sharps, son", he said. "I have no use for it any more and it's plumb useful for throwing a scare into some fellows of the kind you're likely meet in your line of work." So I carried the gun around chiefly to scare some of the hardcases who'd like to have tangled with me. It made them think twice.'

Cardigan blew out his cheeks. 'Hell, you had a gunslinger's reputation. That should have scared them plenty.'

'Yes, but I didn't enjoy that reputation,' admitted Travers. 'I kind of collected it without trying. Then it got bigger, especially after my run-in with the Kloots and Cass Chisnall in Wyoming. I never relished smoking it out with anyone. I'll admit to being scared deep down every time I got into gunplay. Any intelligent man would be.'

'But I guess there was always some wet-behind-the-ears kid, who figured on taking out Keever, the gunslick town marshal of Apache Wells,' commented Cardigan.

'Sure, but when they saw me patrolling the street with that gun in my fist, they wised up pretty quick. Oh, I could always back my reputation with a sixgun when it was called for, but I'd far sooner keep the peace without any shooting. The fact is I tested that carbine at first to see if it was in working order but I never fired it in anger until I came into this country and Wallis and Twigg tried to backshoot me. I'm none too fond of it, either. It's too heavy and cumbersome.'

'Well, I'll be damned!' breathed Cardigan. 'I figured you were a past master in using it and I reckon all this country has the same notion.'

Travers gave a wry smile. 'You can accuse me of some play-acting with that weapon as a stage prop – though it sure came in useful when the chips were down. Now, it belongs in the past – like Will Keever.'

*

Later that day with the sun spreading spring warmth over the land where the now freed creek flowed without hindrance, the buffalo gun made a swift arc through the air over the watercourse. Standing on the bank, the lone man who was once known as Will Keever grinned contentedly as it created a satisfying splash and sank beneath the surface.

Then he turned, mounted his horse and rode towards the TT ranch house. This invigorating day, he thought, promised excellent conditions for the forthcoming round-up with which the TT outfit would inaugurate its new start.